LONDON MONUMENT

THE THAMES

LONDON

FLIGHTS
AND
CHIMES
AND
Mysterious
TIMES

FLIGHTS
AND
CHIMES
AND
Mysterious TIMES

Emma Trevayne

ILLUSTRATIONS BY GLENN THOMAS

Simon & Schuster Books for Young Readers

NEW YORK   LONDON   TORONTO   SYDNEY   NEW DELHI

SIMON & SCHUSTER BOOKS FOR YOUNG READERS
An imprint of Simon & Schuster Children's Publishing Division
1230 Avenue of the Americas, New York, New York 10020

SIMON & SCHUSTER BOOKS FOR YOUNG READERS is a trademark of Simon & Schuster, Inc.

For information about special discounts for bulk purchases, please contact Simon & Schuster Special Sales at 1-866-506-1949 or business@simonandschuster.com.

The Simon & Schuster Speakers Bureau can bring authors to your live event. For more information or to book an event, contact the Simon & Schuster Speakers Bureau at 1-866-248-3049 or visit our website at www.simonspeakers.com.

Jacket design by Lizzy Bromley
Map illustrations by Drew Willis
Interior design by Hilary Zarycky
The text for this book is set in Granjon.
The illustrations for this book are rendered digitally.
Manufactured in the United States of America
0414 FFG
2 4 6 8 10 9 7 5 3 1
Library of Congress Cataloging-in-Publication Data
Trevayne, Emma.
Flights and chimes and mysterious times / Emma Trevayne.—First edition.
    pages cm
Summary: In nineteenth century London, Jack Foster discovers a mysterious mechanical world he may never escape.
ISBN 978-1-4424-9877-8 (hardcover)
ISBN 978-1-4424-9880-8 (eBook)
[1. Fairy tales.] I. Title.
PZ8.T772Fl 2014
[Fic]—dc23
2013019389

FIRST
EDITION

To every reader who believes in legends and doorways
To every writer whose stories have let me explore them
And to Brooks, the very first to believe in these ones

ACKNOWLEDGMENTS

Many people were instrumental in helping the Gearwing—as this story was known for several months—take the long flight from imagination to reality. Undying thanks to:

My family, for love, encouragement, earwigs, and pineapples.

Brittany and Brie, who keep me sane.

Brooks Sherman, extraordinary agent and even better friend, to whom this book is partly dedicated because the idea hatched after a conversation with him and because he refused to let me give up when I got discouraged. No "thank you" could ever be enough. More gratitude to the rest of FinePrint, particularly Janet, to Kathleen Ortiz and all at New Leaf Literary & Media, and always, always to Meredith Barnes.

My editor, Zareen Jaffery, who needed exactly a minute and a half of our first phone call to convince me that the Gearwing's delicate mechanisms would be safe—and run more smoothly—in her capable hands. Zareen, thank you for your passion and serenity. You absolutely hang the moon, and thus worlds both real and imagined are immeasurably brighter when you're part of them. Everyone at S&S BFYR, including (but in no way limited to) Justin Chanda and the whole editorial team for supporting the book, and designer Lizzy Bromley, who made it so beautiful I just want to hug her forever. Lizzy literally searched across the world, all the way to Australia, to find Glenn Thomas, whose illustrations still make me gasp in wonder. Glenn, we've never met and yet you not only managed to see inside my head and bring the pictures there to life, you improved on them. That was some trick. Thank you so, so much.

Those marvelous people who run London's museums and historic attractions, without which the story would have had infinitely less depth and detail. Any mistakes are my fault, any liberties are taken only where necessary.

Bradley who read a rough draft when he was precisely Jack's age, and Tonya, who read it with him.

Katherine Catmull for brightening my days far more often than she knows, Claire Legrand for sharing everything from editors to guacamole with me, and especially Stefan Bachmann, my fellow clockwork bird enthusiast, for a peculiar friendship.

*"Hope is the thing with feathers
that perches in the soul."*

—EMILY DICKINSON

Prologue

THERE ARE DOORWAYS, AND THERE are *door-ways*.

Of the first type, there are many: into bedrooms and shops, schools and houses and parlors. Most people spend their lives going in and out of the first kind, slamming them on occasion, or else closing them with the softest of little *snicks*. They never know of the second kind, and depending on the type of person they are, they might be glad of this, or not.

London, in those days, had too many of the first to count, and that wasn't nearly as many as there are now. Shut tight against the oily black soot that hung over the city like the permanent promise of rain, or thrown open to tempt any fresh breeze that might wander in off the river as if it were coming to tea.

Behind the nicer ones, whose knockers gleamed from the housekeeper's daily polish, electric lights shone. In the grotty East End slums, the barest hint of glow from tallow candles oozed out from gaps around the wood. In the heart of the city, people gathered in dank alleys for a glimpse of the star just seen on the stage as she stepped through and out to her waiting carriage. Behind them all, people went about their business, whatever honorable or thieving business that was.

Of the second type, there were far fewer, and only one that matters for this tale.

Those who knew enough looked for them, but not in the right places. They searched graveyards, and in dim, shuttered rooms where people gathered in circles to clasp hands. Others scorned them for the attempt. What a thing for sensible people to do! And London, seat of the mighty British Empire, should be sensible above all things. But the queen herself was one of those who looked for doorways into the realm of the dead, never finding one, and certainly never stumbling across an entrance to a different world where the people were very much alive.

There were legends, of course. Stories from faraway lands, changing and growing from one country to the next.

The landscape always changed, but the magic never did. The tales were told to children wrapped up in sheets, to frighten or soothe, but those doing the telling didn't have to believe. Perhaps it was just as well that they didn't, for the stories got so much of it wrong. They always do. The legends told of dragons and faeries, of locked towers and imprisoned princesses, and this was true enough.

But the faeries didn't come in hues of blue and pink. They did not smile, except when something went wrong. Black, silver, brown, and tarnished copper are the things to be thought of here. They oiled one another regularly, as girls might plait one another's hair, and their laughter rang like steel. Dragons curled like smoke in hidden caves, breathing steam, not fire.

There were people, too, normal except that they weren't, not really. Occasionally they escaped through a door, bringing with them knowledge that seemed like magic, for to them that was the same as science, and they learned from their creatures.

And there was one thing that was not a faery or a dragon, though it had wings, one thing that was even more magical.

Or it was, before it was broken. Before it was killed.

But some things don't stay dead forever.

CHAPTER ONE

The Sorcerer Ever Watchful

London, 1899

WHEN LORCAN WALKED, HE DID so deliberately, slowly, as if to gauge just how deeply his fine shoes sank into the mud.

Mostly, he preferred to sit. Sitting was for those in command, walking for the commanded. It wasn't often that he walked, but when told to, he went.

For there was only one who could give such orders, and to refuse her would be unthinkable. Unforgivable.

Right now, he was walking, not far, though *far* was relative. He was a long way from home and wished to be back, but the Lady wanted a boy, a son, and the Lady got her every wish.

Hard as he'd tried to delay, the inevitable time had

come. That blasted doctor's experiments to find another solution had all failed. The cats and birds and butterflies he'd fetched to please her had grown tiresome and been set free from the palace to run rampant outside. And so Lorcan carved his way through busy streets in the wrong place, so familiar and yet so strange.

Small metal things jangled in his pockets with every step, making his long fingers twitch with desire to stop them. Instead, he stroked his mustache and watched the people rushing past. They paid him little notice on their way to and from the trains. If they marked him at all, it was for the strangeness of his dark glasses, but it was bright here, lurid and blinding with its electric lights. Billows of steam dropped soot on traveling clothes and this, at least, eased his longing to be back in his own land.

Soon, very soon. A whistle blew, high, screeching, so like a frightened birdcall that his fingers jerked toward his pocket again. This time he let them, just to check, and they caught on a half-dozen sharp edges.

Yes, still there.

Lorcan drew out a smooth, heavy golden watch on a long chain as he stopped in the middle of the station, pretending it was what he'd meant to do all along. "*Patience,*" whispered the filigreed hands. Not this one, but the next.

It would be so very simple. The plan was in place, and

the Lady would be pleased, pleased with Lorcan for a job well done.

Perhaps she would smile. It had been some time since she'd truly smiled, yet longer since Lorcan had been brought to her by the one who came before him, just as he'd do with the boy. The man who'd taken him was dead now, rotted to dust. Lorcan could not remember his name.

He'd been young then, and happy as boys should be. But he had aged, aged so he could be her son no more, and with every minute spent on this side of the door he grew older still.

Oh, how he wished to be home. Home, where he'd lived thousands of days and no longer aged a single one.

He felt, once again, for his pocket.

The train withdrew from the platform with a new set of passengers, headed north to where the sky was cold, stars frozen behind a shield of clouds.

"Five minutes," teased the timepiece. Soon, yes, he could return, back to the land of comforting things. A home where he was powerful, for he had scant power here. The Lady would be amused by her new child, and the fleets needed his attention. It was unlikely they'd fallen into disrepair in his absence, but war rumbled across the ocean like thunder before a storm. The colonies wished to govern themselves and would soon need a reminder that there was only one

Empire and only one Lady to rule it. There, the objects in his pockets would settle once again into their safe, hidden place. He disliked carrying them and did so only out of fear.

A new wave of people brushed past, tickets clutched in their hands. It was easy to tell the ones who made regular journeys by their surefooted trots to the correct platforms, papers tucked under their arms, corners of leather satchels worn from use. Others were tentative, slow as they read their tickets over and over, or else looked to the uniformed station inspector for help. This, he gave, pointing meaty arms in the right direction, brass buttons gleaming and strained on his chest. His eye caught Lorcan's and he smiled affably, seemingly assuming Lorcan was waiting to greet someone off the two-seventeen.

Which was true, in its way.

Two minutes.

One.

He heard it before he saw it, the *chug-chug* of the engine. If there'd been a normal heart in his chest, it would have changed to match the pace exactly, but he did not have a normal heart. Here, it could be said, he barely had a thing that could be termed a heart, simply a dead, useless lump in its place.

The train crawled into view, slowly swallowing the tracks as if it were tired and hungry from its long journey and, after it had eaten, could rest with its black nose nudged up to the end of the platform. It gave a great, wheezy sigh, steam filling the station as the doors clanked open. Ghostly shapes of gentlemen helped ladies step down without turning an ankle.

He moved closer.

"Hurry up, Jack," said a woman.

"Yes, Mother."

Lorcan cared nothing for what this would do to the woman, who was a fool. Sending her son away to school, fetching him only for holidays that interfered with the lavish parties she threw for trivial reasons.

Not like the Lady, who would keep the boy Jack close, spoiling him with love and trinkets and cake, for all children enjoy cake.

It was inconvenient to do it this way, but Lorcan's feet had sunk into the mud outside the high walls of the school, toes curled in frustration that there was no way to lure the boy out. No way to tell him he would be taken to a better place, to the Lady, to be the next son of the Empire of Clouds. And this way did have some benefits.

There he was.

Jack looked like the Lady, the same dark hair and eyes, the same smooth skin, though his had a smattering of freckles across the nose, which Lorcan knew would delight her. He was slightly short for his age, but healthy otherwise, a robust pinkness to his cheeks. Suit creased in the way of all young boys, the tail of a black- and blue-striped tie peeking from his satchel, the toes of his shoes shined to mirror-glass.

A perfect choice, and Lorcan had put in too much effort to stop now. Months, it had taken him. Months of watching, deciding, waiting, and the time he had been given was nearly up.

If Lorcan was reduced to parlor tricks and a few well-placed lies to obtain him, so be it. It was a small sacrifice, and there was none too large to please the Lady.

"Stay here while I see to your things and arrange for a hansom. Your father needed Wilson and the carriage today," said the fool, her elegant green dress fluttering as she left him—left him!—alone. Lorcan smiled, holding his breath until she was arranging for a porter to carry those possessions the boy felt he couldn't do without for a short time.

Well, those could be replaced. He wouldn't need them, in any case, not where he was going.

Lorcan's hands twitched again. Tempting, so tempting, simply to grab the boy and run, but he had not gotten this far without patience. There was always the chance he would be caught, however small, and were that to happen, he would never make it home to the Lady.

Anything for the Lady. Nothing and nobody mattered more.

He gritted his teeth. He must do this; he had no choice.

The fool returned. She and Jack followed a trolley containing two small trunks, pushed by a uniformed man thin as a fiend. Lorcan let them get ahead, but not too far.

No, not too far.

He watched them climb into a cab, the fool's nose wrinkled, the boy's eyes alight with this rare adventure. The driver snapped the reins against a scrubby nag, which whinnied and snorted before pulling away.

A distasteful mode of transport, to be sure, but it could not be avoided. Lorcan hailed one of his own, giving an address in Mayfair he'd known for some time now.

The great clock tower at Westminster boomed across the city, marking the half hour. Lorcan jumped. It shouldn't— Then he remembered.

It was a beautiful tower, brown stone and iron, an enormous, lovely clock. They had a name for the bell here. Big Ben, they called it. Ridiculous. He'd stolen every detail of the tower except that one.

He patted his pockets again, leaned back against the filthy cushions, and smiled.

Oh, the Lady would be so pleased.

CHAPTER TWO

Lies & Spies

JACK FOSTER SAT ON THE grass in the garden, beyond the creeping reach of the house's shadow, wishing he were somewhere else. Anywhere would be less dull than this house to which he was confined for the summer holidays.

It was an old house and very grand. The sort kept like a precious jewel, polished when necessary, and worn—comfortably or not—on the shoulders of the sons and daughters who inherited it. Ivy climbed the facade, hacked away from the windows by the gardener with a pair of wickedly sharp shears Jack had been forbidden ever to touch. Little boys had lost fingers, said Mrs. Pond. However much Jack bristled at being called a little boy, for he was nearly eleven, the thought made him shiver. The blood, and a thing squirming wormlike on the ground.

In his imagination, they could always still move.

The clock in the hall chimed, loud enough to be heard outdoors. Jack opened his mouth as if to speak, and waited, an eye on the kitchen window.

"Come inside, Jack, and have some cake."

Mrs. Pond was very punctual. Jack did not want cake. He wanted the rich, brown food at school, with its mysterious pieces of meat swimming in murky sludge, but he'd not dare say such a thing to Mrs. Pond. She was allowed to punish him, after all, and she wouldn't understand why he was homesick for such an unappetizing meal.

"All right," he called, loud enough that she'd hear him through the open kitchen window, not so loud as to disturb his mother and her guests.

He got to his feet, dragging them through the short grass as if they were forged from the metals that made his father so wealthy. Closer to the house, the scent of roasting lamb washed over him, almost a shadow in itself, dark and thick, and it made him cold to stand in. *Little boys* would be in bed by the time it was served to guests at the long table, the new electric lights bouncing off diamonds and feathers. Laughter would climb the stairs, tiptoe down the hallway to slither through the crack beneath his bedroom door. Later still, when the plates were cleared away, shoes would trample between the dining room and the conservatory, where Jack's mother would play the piano he'd once gotten into so much trouble for trying to take apart, just to see how it worked.

A knock sounded. Another visitor. Servants and tradesmen came in around the back, pressing a bell for entrance. Jack flattened himself to the wall, out of sight, as the maid hurried into the corridor that ran the length of the house, down the middle, widening to a large hall at the front door. Laughter came from the parlor set off to one side. Clumsy, stupid fingers fumbled with the locks. Jack hadn't bothered to learn this one's name. She'd be gone soon, as fast as the others, just as soon as she upset Mother over some tiny thing. Mother was quite in the habit of sending people away.

"A very good afternoon to you," said the man at the door. Weak sunlight spread around him, so to Jack he was just a shadow, a dark outline, face featureless. Leaves blew in with him, curled like feathers, though it was summer and the trees should not be shedding yet.

And when Jack had been outside, there'd been no wind. A trick, then.

His voice was odd, though Jack couldn't describe, precisely, what made it so. "I have been invited by the . . ." The man paused. The parlor door opened.

"You'll be Mr. Havelock, of whom we've heard such

marvelous things," said Jack's mother. "Do come in. We're gathered in the parlor. Your correspondence said no more than a half dozen, and I assure you, they are all sympathetic. Verity, please see to the gentleman's coat. The parlor is dreadfully warm today."

"Thank you, madam," said Mr. Havelock. The door snapped shut. His shoes clicked on the floor, which was laid out like a checkerboard. Years earlier, Jack had tried to play a proper game of chess on it, but he had only normal-sized pieces, and one of Mrs. Pond's sturdy shoes had sent two crucial pawns skittering as she carried a tray full of tea things into the parlor.

Mr. Havelock stood on a black tile, with his suit and fine leather case to match. Not like a king, thought Jack, but a rook, perhaps, tall and straight-shouldered. He was young—thirty at most—and his face was very smooth, with just a neat little mustache and beard to mar it. A small pair of spectacles covered his eyes, the oddest thing. Possibly he had some kind of ailment that called for the darkened lenses. Possibly he just wished to appear mysterious.

Verity moved to take Mr. Havelock's thin coat. His arms were just free of the sleeves, a silk waistcoat revealed, when his hands jerked violently, making to grab the coat back. In shock, the maid dropped the thing, a half-dozen small bits of metal tumbling from the pockets to spill and roll over the floor.

One hit the toe of Jack's shoe in his hiding place, and he picked it up. It was nothing, a small bolt, filmed with rust. But it seemed of some import to Mr. Havelock, who was busy gathering up the others as Mrs. Foster scolded Verity for her clumsiness.

"Apologies," said Mr. Havelock tightly. "Tools of the trade. I must keep them with me. Metal is essential. For its grounding properties, you understand."

"Of course," said Mrs. Foster, who clearly did *not* understand. "You've found them all?"

Mr. Havelock nodded. A smile flashed, quick and cold. "The child has one."

Jack started, disturbing the shadows. From behind the smoky glass, Mr. Havelock stared right at him. His spine tingled.

"Jack?" his mother said, following Mr. Havelock's gaze. He stepped out into the light, safe from her sharp tongue while there was a guest present. "What *are* you doing, sneaking around like that? Do they not teach manners at that school of yours? And do give Mr. Havelock back his . . . whatever it is."

Or not so safe.

"Now, now, nothing wrong with curiosity! Come,

young man. Jack, you say?" His mother nodded. "Lorcan Havelock, at your service."

Jack still could not see his eyes. His smile, though wide, pressed his lips to whiteness between the beard and mustache. His fingers twitched, as if reaching for the pocket watch that hung from a thick golden chain on his vest, but he let them fall to his side without checking the hour.

"Nice to meet you, sir," said Jack. A proper greeting to please his mother. He held out the bolt.

"Yes." A whisper, barely heard. The spectacles were like black, black eyes, staring at Jack. "Yes," said Mr. Havelock, louder now, taking the bolt with cold fingers.

"You're a magician," said Jack.

The man's other hand curled, crushing the brim of his hat. He smiled that thin-lipped smile again, and then it widened into something real. "But of course," said Mr. Havelock, casting about until his eyes lit upon a vase filled with flowers picked by Mrs. Pond just that morning. He plucked one out, a big, fresh, yellow daisy, and Jack watched as, at Mr. Havelock's touch, it wilted in seconds, petals falling dry and brown onto the floor. Jack gasped, but oh, that wasn't the best of it. At a snap of the magician's fingers, the petals rose, rejoined, bloomed back into brightness, and Jack stumbled backward.

"Do excuse him," Mrs. Foster said. "His education is

dreadfully mundane. His father's choice, you know. Mr. Havelock is our new *spiritualist*," she said to Jack. "Highly recommended by the Society. And we simply must get started. Run along, and tell Mrs. Pond not to oversalt the meat."

He wouldn't.

"The child won't be joining us?" asked Mr. Havelock, tucking the fresh, beautiful flower back in with the rest.

Mrs. Foster laughed. "Oh, no. This way, please."

Mr. Havelock moved, slowly, stare unwavering. It made Jack want to fidget, but he stayed still.

She led Mr. Havelock into the parlor, closing tight the door on exclamations, introductions, her friends like chattering birds, lofty in their trees of wealth and leisure.

There wasn't much time. Too soon, Mrs. Pond would come looking for him, a thrashing promised for not coming when called, though she never did it. Bootlaces curled like snakes on the tile, left behind as he padded across the floor, silent, to crouch on his knees, press his eye to the keyhole.

Inside was dark as night, a single candle on a table the one winking star. Heavy velvet curtains had been drawn, and seven straight-backed chairs sat in a circle on the edge of the faint pool of light. If he squinted, he could just make out parts of Mother and Mr. Havelock facing the door, but the rest were just blurs of elegance, as her friends had always been to him.

"Not *everything* has a soul, surely," said one of them, in a voice like thick treacle. "Why, these diamonds are beautiful, but they are not *alive*."

"Oh?"

A glittering hairpin, shaped as a bird, took off from her head to swoop once around the room. Jack fell back from the keyhole, and by the time he righted himself, the bird had returned to her hair, perfectly still and ordinary.

A few of the women tittered. Mr. Havelock leaned forward, the spectacles shimmering darkly, as if they were catching the candle smoke, trapping it within.

"A parlor trick," he said. "In fact, you are right, good woman, but most things do. Regardless, we are not here to summon the souls of your pretty jewels, even if they had them."

More tittering.

"Concentration is essential if the spirits are to cooperate!" he said. Jack turned his head to press his ear to the keyhole. Mr. Havelock sounded . . . angry. Angry at the silly giggles and trying to hide it.

Footsteps tapped in the kitchen. Mrs. Pond was coming. He wouldn't get to see anything interesting, which just wasn't fair at all. Even Mr. Havelock had asked if Jack would be joining the summoning, but Mother didn't want him.

"You must be dedicated to your goal," said Mr. Havelock sternly. "Willing to do whatever is required to obtain that which you seek." Not angry now. Jack peered through the keyhole again. Now Mr. Havelock sounded like a thirsty man who had just had a glass of wine set before him. A solemn cloud hung over the table.

The kitchen door opened.

Mr. Havelock's head snapped up, looking past the women, right to the keyhole. Jack blinked, scrambling back on the chessboard tiles, sure it had been a trick of the light. An errant flick of the candle from an unstoppered draft, catching the dark glass and making Mr. Havelock's eyes flash with flame. A trick of the light, he thought, as Mrs. Pond hoisted him by the elbow to drag him away.

Jack's bedroom was large and blue and hadn't changed at all since he'd been a baby, except that a bed stood where his cradle used to be. Other rooms went from green to white to hideous floral wallpapers at his mother's whim, but this she left alone. Or simply forgot. It had been his grandfather's room once, long ago, but Jack had never met him and didn't know if it'd been different back then.

Bookshelves of fairy stories, dictionaries, and the kind

of thick tomes that people feel they should read but never do lined one of the walls. Jack had, in fact, read most of them, but the fairy stories were his favorites, filled with dragons and unicorns and phoenixes and princes with swords who saved the land.

Windows took up another wall, rows of toys the rest of the space not occupied by his bed. His favorites were the toy soldiers that had once belonged to his father, mixed in with newer ones so Jack could build proper armies of age and rank. Young corporals who did all the fighting under the direction of colonels who would be fat if not for that they were made of wood. He wondered if they did have souls, like Mr. Havelock said.

The room had taken on a dusty, unused air since Jack went off to school, only slightly stirred by his return for various holidays. A school trunk stood empty by the wardrobe, ready to be filled again. Headmaster Adams and the rest of Jack's teachers might be strict in their quest to raise decent, educated, upstanding young men, ready for the rigors of London business and society, but he slept better there, in the dormitory he shared with five other boys, than in this big, lonely room he had all to himself.

"Come downstairs, Jack, and no dawdling, mind," Mrs. Pond called from the landing below. More cake, he was sure. She was already returning to the kitchen when he left his dull room for the dull, darkly paneled stairway, her round body and snow-white head descending down through the dull, dull house.

"Hands washed," she commanded, wiping her own plump ones on a floury apron. He was already lathering the soap, making sure to clean his fingernails because she was watching.

A loud thump echoed through the house. Mrs. Pond clicked her tongue but said nothing.

"Do you think that was a ghost?" Jack asked.

"I think you should eat your cake and drink your milk."

He took a bite. The kitchen glowed with a lucky shaft of sun, determined enough to break through the gray haze ever present over the city, particularly in summer.

Mr. Havelock was in the parlor again, as he had been many days since that first. Jack caught glimpses of him, but always felt that tingle down his back, as if he were the one being watched with fiery eyes. Every time, the spiritualist asked Jack's mother if the boy would be taking part. Every time, she said no.

Another thump. The chatelaine hanging from Mrs. Pond's waist jangled as she shuddered, keys and scissors and thimble swinging.

Perhaps she was frightened of them, but they didn't

frighten Jack. It was interesting, the talk of ghosts and spirits and other worlds.

He liked the idea. There was always the chance those worlds were more interesting than this one.

Wisely, he didn't say so to Mrs. Pond.

"Your mother would like to know why the gramophone isn't working."

Jack shrugged. "A ghost must've got to it."

At this, Mrs. Pond smiled in the way that turned her face to an apple left to soften too long. "None of that cheek, you, and fix it."

"I will," said Jack sulkily. They'd all be grateful when the needle stopped wobbling. "When will Father be home?" He was careful not to say he had nothing to do; Mrs. Pond had some very tedious ways of keeping him amused, like shining the silver.

"Not until the party," she said, "and you aren't to disturb them. Baroness Watson is coming, and such a job I've had getting everything up to scratch for royalty, I can tell you." She turned back to a chopping board full of vegetables, a large knife in her hand.

Royalty. Well, la-di-da. Jack didn't see what made them so special. Sitting around all day with a crown on one's head couldn't be particularly difficult. Perhaps the crown was heavy and they went to bed with aching heads every evening.

Behind the parlor door, someone screamed, another laughed. The knife struck—*thwack, thwack*—potato slices falling to either side. Jack toyed with the crumbs on his plate.

A loud buzzing filled the room. "Oh, my stars!" Mrs. Pond said this every time. Sometimes, she would mutter, "*Infernal contraption*," beneath her breath when she thought no one could hear. Knife in hand, she crossed the kitchen to a bank of round buttons set into the wall, pressing the one for the parlor. The light behind it faded to nothing. "Verity!"

"Coming, marm." The maid burst through the cellar door, brushing grime from her apron, and hurried out to the parlor.

Good-byes filtered in as the ladies, full of an afternoon's amusement, set off to their own homes, husbands, and children. Jack heard his mother promising tea on this day or that, or excursions to the new milliner about whom everyone was saying such complimentary things. He waited for Verity to return, dart back to her business in the cellar, and made his own way to the parlor, for he had not seen his mother since breakfast.

But she was not alone.

Voices spilled through the closed door, poured from the keyhole. Jack put his eye to it, as he did so often, to see her wringing her hands, large rings glinting in the light from the open drapes.

"He has always been an odd child," she said. Jack scowled. He was *not* odd. Just because she liked to spend her time giggling with other silly women rather than read or play chess and thought tinkering with clocks and gramophones was a job for common workmen ... And how would she know he was odd, even if he were? She had sent him away to school. She scarcely saw him.

"Of course, of course," said Mr. Havelock soothingly. "I detected it the moment I saw him. You understand that naturally this would make him a good candidate."

"An apprenticeship, you say?"

Jack thought his ears might pop clean from his head, so hard was he straining to hear.

"He would be well taken care of," said Mr. Havelock, so silkily that Jack's mother did not seem to notice it wasn't quite an answer to her question. She paced the room, moving in and out of view from the keyhole. A swish of purple velvets and lace, back and forth.

"Clearly the movement is only gaining strength," she said. "Why, the Society counts among its number a vast array of influential, prominent persons, myself included, if you will excuse me."

"Quite, madam. He would witness untold mysteries,

secrets permitted to only a fortunate few from this world."

Mrs. Foster wrung her hands again, squeezing the air from Jack's lungs through the keyhole. Did she want to send him away again, somewhere new, to learn from Mr. Havelock, who said he wasn't a magician but Jack was not so sure?

"Sadly, my husband, while indulgent, isn't nearly so forward-thinking as ourselves." She turned from the window, so Jack could see her face, pretty, distant. "Far more concerned with the material, the tangible. No," she said, shaking her head. "I mustn't. His father would be furious. Generations of Fosters have attended that school, successes every one." Her back straightened.

"I assure you—" Mr. Havelock began.

"No," she said. "Strange he may be, but he will stay where he is."

Mr. Havelock did not like this. Jack squinted. Those dark glasses shielded the eyes, but not the tightening of Mr. Havelock's jaw, the thinning of his lips below his mustache. "You are making a grave error, madam," he said, and his voice was not silky now. It was a voice with teeth trying not to bite.

"I expect so," she answered, cool and brittle. "It would not be the first."

He nodded once. His hat lay on the table beside the single candle, snuffed and smoking, and he picked it up.

Jack scrambled from the door, to the stairs. All the way up he ran, not stopping or caring who heard his thumping, rushing footsteps. She did not want him here, but that was not so very unusual—Jack's room at school was full of boys whose parents felt thus—but nor would she allow him to learn something truly interesting, more so than maths and Dickens and silly history, as if it mattered a whit what this king or that once said atop a hill. The one time he actually *wished* to be sent away, and she wouldn't do it. As if she knew and wanted to spite him.

Jack pushed his face into his pillow and hated her.

CHAPTER THREE

Twelve of the Clock

THE SKY GREW NEARLY DARK as he lay on his bed, waiting for Mrs. Pond to bring his supper on a tray. The toy soldiers gathered a few more flakes of dust on their shelves; the books stayed shut and squeezed together, telling their stories only to themselves between their covers.

The landing creaked, but it was not Mrs. Pond who pushed the door open with her back, hands full of milk, boiled eggs, toast. Jack sat up. Mrs. Foster, lovely in a blue silk dress, stepped inside. She was coming to say she'd changed her mind, and Jack's heart lifted until he remembered that she didn't know he'd heard the conversation at all.

"Hello, darling," she said, staying close to the door, head cocked, listening for the first guests to arrive. "Your clothes are getting too small. I don't know how I didn't notice. Mrs. Pond will take you to the outfitters tomorrow."

"Why won't you take me?" he asked. "Or Father?"

His mother smiled with very red lips and patted her hair. "Your father has to work, of course."

"He doesn't have to," said Jack. "We are rich enough." The Foster family had traded in valuable metals for a very long time, metals that built ships and formed rings around ladies' fingers.

"Don't be crass," snapped Mrs. Foster. "The company is a proud family tradition, and it will one day be yours. You should be grateful your father works so hard." Her voice softened. "And I would take you myself, darling—you know that—but I promised Mrs. Hamilton I would visit before they leave for the continent. Poor Eleanor. She's had such a difficult time of it recently, what with her father . . . At any rate," she said, touching a hand to her hair again, "you'll go with Mrs. Pond, and mind you listen to her. No running off."

"Yes, Mother," he said, lying down and turning his head to the window. She would not punish him, not now. She couldn't spare the time.

"Honestly! These moods of yours, I don't know from where they come."

She was always worried about moods. And that he was *odd*. Her sister had been put in an asylum because of moods and had died there. They never spoke of her, but Mrs. Pond told him the story once when he'd found a photograph of a woman he didn't recognize.

"Good night, Jack."

"Good night, Mother."

He did not see her, or Father, the following morning. It was a leaden day, a gathering gloom of clouds low over the house, but rain couldn't dampen his excitement for an outing. Even for something as tedious as shopping. Mrs. Pond called enough instructions to Verity to keep the girl busy for a whole week as Jack ate breakfast in large bites. He stood on the checkered floor, a little pawn, for a full five minutes before Mrs. Pond joined him, a large bag over one arm, apron gone from her proper brown dress.

A pair of black horses, gleaming, stomping restlessly, stood in front of a carriage on the street. Curtains hung at windows cut into the doors, an ironwork step just below. Lanterns were fixed on either side of a bench, high and open to the air. The horses' eyes flickered to the house, the road, the great green park opposite. A sea of trees and grass surrounding the famous Serpentine, where Mrs. Pond sometimes took Jack to feed the ducks, its waters steel gray under the stormy sky. Out of sight at the northern corner stood the towering Marble Arch, white stone choked by soot and grime.

"Oxford Street, if you please, Wilson," said Mrs. Pond to the man on the bench, leather reins loose in his equally leathery fist. "A hair shy of Tottenham Court Road, and do try to avoid getting mired in that mess at Grosvenor Square."

"Right you are, Effie," said Wilson, jumping down. "Hullo, young Jack." Wilson was a big man, more like a boxer than a merchant's trusted servant, playing dress up in a suit stretched to bursting over his muscles, a top hat shadowing his pockmarked face. "Home for the holidays, eh? Glad to be back?"

"Er," said Jack. Thunder rumbled to the west, and Mrs. Pond nudged him to the carriage door.

"We'd best be off. I don't much like the sound of that. Up you go, Jack." Wilson closed the door the moment they settled on the seats and climbed easily back to his bench. The horses, overeager and snorting, took off with a jolt at the barest snap of leather on their flanks, along narrow streets lined with tall, sugar-confection houses.

Carriages rattled over cobblestones, pulled by horses of every color. Here and there, Jack caught a glimpse of a motorcar and pressed his face to the window until it was out of sight. Mr. Foster sometimes hinted at buying one, but Mrs. Foster would mutter things about *those beastly machines* not being safe until he dropped the subject.

Mrs. Pond sat on the opposite seat, a large bag beside her on the plush red velvet. Knitting needles clicked and flashed, churning out row after row of neat stitches. The goings-on of the city didn't seem to interest her nearly as much as they fascinated Jack.

"How much longer?" asked Jack, who wanted to be out among all the people, not trapped inside the shaking, stuffy carriage. Smoke curled upward behind spiky roofs as they traveled down crooked streets like rainwater finding a crack, flowing until they reached the end and it spat them out, into another crack.

"Nearly there," she answered, not looking up.

But, in fact, it was nearly half an hour before Wilson managed to urge the carriage through the traffic to their destination, through a London Jack barely knew, though his father spoke of it as the world's greatest city, the seat of the most magnificent empire ever to stand.

Street vendors in grubby trousers hawked ice creams and glasses of sherbet; uniformed maids scurried through their errands. They passed a music hall where, on a rare outing—a birthday treat two years previously—Jack had watched from a box as acrobats in striped tights flew through the air and a medium with a cloth over her eyes predicted the contents of people's pockets. A magician had levitated a vase only to send it smashing to the ground. As the audience booed and laughed, the shards turned to butterflies that fluttered up to the rafters.

He'd begged and begged to be allowed back the following night, but his parents refused, saying too much excitement would spoil him. Now the place was dark, empty, the performers still slumbering in their beds.

And his mother wouldn't let him go with Mr. Havelock to learn even better tricks than those.

Because he was odd, but not odd enough.

"Have you eaten a lemon, child? Cheer up. We might find some way to amuse ourselves for an hour or two if we're not long getting you kitted out."

And, indeed, it took no time at all—or so it seemed—for a pile of shirts that were too loose, trousers three inches too long, and jumpers that scratched at his neck to pile on the counter in the shop. An old, bald man with bugged eyes promised to send his boy out with the delivery the very next day, just as soon as the needlewoman had finished with them. Jack gazed at a small wooden compass, edges bound with brass, until Mrs. Pond added it to the bill.

"That's a lovely thing," said Mrs. Pond. "Don't lose it, mind."

"I won't." Jack had never lost anything in his life except on purpose, which cheated the rule of lost things. Sometimes it was simply easier to misplace a toy or a hat than to tell Mother he did not like her gift.

Outside, Wilson was chasing away an urchin with big eyes for the horses, the bits of ribbon and silver on their bridles. Grubby, rail thin, the wretch slipped around a fruit stall to be swallowed by the city in one meager mouthful.

"Rascal," scoffed Wilson, returning to where Jack waited with Mrs. Pond. "Home, Effie?"

She looked at the sky. Still the color of old ghosts, haunting the streets and spires from above, but no worse than it had been an hour before. "The Embankment," she decided. "We'll have an early lunch, and Jack—"

"Can see the boats!" said Jack, grinning so hard his face might split and earning himself a halfhearted cuff around the ear.

"Don't interrupt, you. Off we go."

The gardens, not yet crisp and brown as they would be when the August heat came, cradled a curve of the wide, stinking river. Nannies pushed prams along the curving paths cut into the grass, the babies asleep despite the constant bells, horns, whistles, and shouts that rang out between the ships, carrying over the water. Soot clouded the air and gave white birds black feathers. Below the

walkway, mudlarks scavenged in the shallows for anything to sell, trousers rolled up to their knees.

They left Wilson waiting with the carriage, Mrs. Pond
having been raised, many years before, among the East
End toughs and thus able to do strange and terrible
things with a hat pin should the need arise. Not that anything would, in broad daylight in the genteel, landscaped
greenery.

But it was the boats, rather than the flowers, that drew
Jack's eyes and feet, and he ran as far toward them as he
could get away with before being shouted at. Everything
about them crowed of adventure. The towering masts
holding rippling sails that caught winds blowing across
the world. The curved bows that sliced through water as
if it were air and raced over the seas. He knew all about
them—he'd read a very thick book—but Jack would one
day sit behind his father's desk while other men captained
the ships used by the company, or ones whose engines and
portholes had been forged in its factories.

There were pies and lemonade for lunch, bought from
a man with a barrow near the gates, which tasted like the
food at school. That is to say, they didn't taste of much at
all, and Jack had to chew hard on bits of gristle. He wanted
another, but Mrs. Pond was still carefully eating her first,
sipping lemonade between bites.

"Stay close," she said, wiping gravy from her mouth with a handkerchief. Jack left her on the bench set on the grass, called again by the boats. He slipped among a group of well-dressed folk with odd accents who clustered along the rail, pointing, chattering, words stretched and twanging like violin strings.

"Wouldja lookit that," said one. He raised a pair of brass binoculars. Jack wondered where the people came from, pitying them. London was magnificent.

They began to blather about setting off to climb the Monument, that towering column with its gilded urn atop, dedicated to the terrible fire that once nearly devoured the city, and Jack stopped listening. Mrs. Pond had taken him, once, gasping and wheezing her way up the corkscrew staircase as he ran ahead. It had made him dizzy, and anyway, the funny people were leaving and a steamboat, belching lungfuls of gray, had just blown its horn, ready to chug away to lands unknown.

He looked back. Evidently she had seen a friend, and it was odd to think of Mrs. Pond having friends beyond the bright kitchen from which she bossed the maid about. They were talking, laughing, a toddling child clinging to the other lady's skirts.

The compass weighted his pocket. Jack took it out, touching the fine wood with his thumb, releasing the catch so the lid sprang open. This way and that, he turned, the needle wobbling, always coming to rest with its point to the north.

But something else caught his eye.

Mr. Lorcan Havelock, spiritualist—or magician, as Jack preferred to think—was hurrying along one of the paths through the park. Jack recognized the suit, the hat, the dark glasses most of all.

Mrs. Pond chatted away. Jack hesitated for the space of a breath.

He wanted to know. Know what Mr. Havelock wanted to show him, to teach him. The noise from the river hammered in his ears. Calling out was useless; Mr. Havelock might hear him, but Mrs. Pond would, too.

If Jack could just stop him a little farther away.

He followed.

Twenty paces behind, Jack dodged around the flower beds and prams, the picnickers, and fountains spraying fine clouds of rain.

Mr. Havelock quickened his steps. The Houses of Parliament loomed ahead, pointed roofs like treetops of a stone forest.

"Gracious!"

"Sorry, miss!" Jack said, but he didn't stop.

Ahead, Mr. Havelock passed through the garden gates, into the clamor of carriages and motorcars snarled at the brink of the bridge. Sentinel at the corner of the grand government buildings stood the enormous clock tower everyone called *Big Ben.*

Which was completely, uselessly wrong, irritatingly so. Big Ben was the enormous bell inside, not the clock. The clock was just a clock.

On the other side of a hansom cab pulled by four tall horses, Mr. Havelock's hat—and presumably the rest of him—began to run.

Jack's feet slid in the mud. Someone shouted at him. At some point between spotting Mr. Havelock and the garden gates, Jack had stopped following just because he wanted to speak to the man.

No. A far more interesting question, just at the moment, was where he was going in such a hurry. A meeting?

It could be with anyone. Another magician, perhaps.

But Mr. Havelock stopped, so sharply a nearby horse startled, outside the wrought-iron fence of the Palace of Westminster, where lords in frock coats made their important decisions about running the country.

The clock began to chime. So close, the peal was shockingly loud.

A small gate sliced into the fence, its squeak, if it made one, lost in the cacophony of the bell. Jack felt the gongs in his teeth.

Two.

Three.

The base of the tower was smooth stone, cold as an enemy's smile. Mr. Havelock pressed one velvet-gloved hand to it.

The stone cracked. Cracked neatly, lines growing to meet one another.

A door.

Magician, Jack thought, as Mr. Havelock pushed it open, slipped through. It started to swing shut behind him.

Seven. Eight. And Jack knew in his bones that the door would close, the lines would fade, and it would be gone by the twelfth ring of the bell, because it was magic.

He reached it just as the hinges—if indeed there were any—flattened, the cracks closing.

Perhaps it would not even work for him. Jack wasn't a magician, never would be, because his mother was horrible and never let him do anything.

Ten.

Jack touched the stone. The cracks stuttered, spluttered, regrew. He *was* special, he thought as it opened for him.

Inside was the pitch-black of trapped nighttime, and loud, so loud. Jack clapped his hands to his ears. Overhead, the grand, great bell with its silly name rang twelve o'clock, echoing for an age through the tower and over the rooftops, and then all was still.

CHAPTER FOUR

Londinium, or the Empire
of Clouds

I T REALLY WAS VERY DARK in the clock tower, but Jack
was not afraid of the dark, and anyone who said otherwise was a liar. Bertie Ducksworth at school was a
liar.

"Mr. Havelock?" Now it was Jack's own voice that
rang, but there was no answer.

Blindly, Jack felt his way along the wall. Mr. Havelock
must have a job seeing in here, what with those dark spectacles. Possibly he took them off, folding them neatly into
a pocket so as not to scratch the lenses.

It was daft to have no lamps, no electric lights. Surely
people must come here, clockmakers to set the time and
sweeps with their brooms to clear out the dust, even if

41

the lords in their fancy coats were too busy.

"Hello?" He tried again, but there was no sound, no footsteps, no inconvenient sneeze of someone trying to stay quiet.

The number of times he'd had to pinch his nose to keep his soul in so that he'd make no noise while peering through the parlor keyhole . . .

His face bashed into something very hard, and he said a word for which Mrs. Pond would have given him a proper hiding if she'd been there to hear it. Rubbing his forehead with one hand, Jack flailed about with the other.

The door handle was cold and solidly real in his hand. He turned it. Light began to seep in to the dark room, courtesy of slit-thin windows slashed high in the walls of a square staircase that climbed and climbed into the sky, with small landings on each floor.

Mrs. Pond would still be gossiping with her friend, Wilson chasing urchins away from the horses. It could not be so very high, and if Mr. Havelock was up there, which he must be for there was nowhere else to go, he would be most impressed by Jack's persistence. That, and Jack's magic, for he had opened the door.

"Such talent!" he'd marvel. "Such a special boy I must have to train, and we won't take no for an answer this time!"

The first hundred steps—Jack counted in his head—were easy enough. Then his chest began to burn, making him wish he'd put more effort into games at school, the way the fat games master always shouted at him to.

Up he went, stopping every now and then to breathe, to listen, to test doors that stayed resolutely locked. He thought he could just hear the ticking of the clock, but it could simply be his own heartbeat.

When he certainly must've risen to the stars, a door stood open off the stairs, and his wheezy gasps ceased altogether.

Oh, oh, it was a wondrous thing, better than any gramophone or stinking piano. Every polished gear spun smooth, wheels and pinions oiled, one against another, and the whole thing bigger than Jack himself, bigger than ten of him.

It must be heaps of fun to be a clockmaker, Jack thought. He'd read a very thick book about that, as well.

Tick. Tick. Tick, it commanded to the clock hands you could see from half of London if you tried.

Other than this, the room was entirely still, as if such a grand clock had stolen even the time it took for a dust mote to float across a sunbeam, needing every minute, every second it could find.

But there were no sunbeams. Beyond the high windows, there was only gray. A raindrop hit. Another. Another.

Oh, *blast*.

Jack fairly flew down the stairs, fast as he could without falling, which would do nobody any good.

Mrs. Pond would be *furious*. Such a hiding he'd never seen, surely, and any minute now the great bell would begin to mark the quarter hour, and he'd been gone far too long.

She'd be looking for him to get out of the rain, back into the carriage and home. He could not even say he'd been following Mr. Havelock, who was nowhere to be found, or that the magician made a door appear just where he'd needed one. She would say he was telling tales.

Little boys who wanted their dinner did not tell tales.

Dizzied, he landed at the door to the dark room, and the most terrible thoughts filled his topsy head. What if he couldn't see to make the door? What if it wouldn't appear for him at all?

Well, Mrs. Pond'd have a right time punishing him if he stayed shut up in here forever, so that might not be the worst of things.

Besides, there must be another way out, for the lords and clockmakers and sweeps, ordinary folks unable to wish a door into a wall.

And then disappear.

Jack needn't have worried. After a good bit of fumbling,

he found not only the wall where the door had been, but a handle. Apparently, on this side it pretended to be a real door, but there wasn't much chance to think about that just at the moment. He yanked it open and stepped into a wall of rain.

He was soaked by the time he got to the slippery cobbles, wetter still at the garden gates. "Mrs. Pond!" he yelled into an enormous thunderclap. "Effie!" Which was horribly rude.

No answer came. There was nobody at all, for the rain had cleared the park and the streets around. No carriages or motorcars clogged the entrance to the bridge. Even the ships were just ghostly outlines, decks empty and slick.

His teeth chattered. Water sluiced in his ruined shoes. He could hear Mrs. Pond's voice in his head. "Come inside," it said. "You'll catch your death." She was full of odd expressions Jack never understood. Death wasn't a thing you could trap like an animal.

Quite suddenly, Jack felt enormously alone. It was hard to think, with his brain frozen by cold.

"Wilson!" Wilson would stay. Mrs. Pond would get out of the wet, but Wilson, cap pulled down to his ears, would stay with the horses. Jack simply couldn't see them because they were around a corner, sheltered below a low eave.

Of course. That made sense. His schoolmasters were great

45

ones for things making sense. It just took a bit of thinking.

The rain slowed as Jack made his way along the path, toward the spot where he and Mrs. Pond had left Wilson an age ago. How long, Jack wasn't sure. The clock had surely chimed, its peals swallowed by the storm, but he didn't know when.

A last, stubborn raindrop fell with a *splat* on the top of his head as Jack passed back through the gates and onto the road.

He looked around, squinted, rubbed the water from his eyes.

But the streets were still empty.

After the rain, the city glistened darkly, a forest of chimneys and gables. Black slurry crawled down the gutters. Overhead, a bird gave an experimental, tinny chirp.

The enormity of what he'd done began to weigh on Jack, a coat stitched of fear and stuffed with worry.

He must find a constable or a well-dressed lady to help him find Mrs. Pond, or take him to his father's offices. A hiding didn't feel so much of a frightening thing as it had before.

A man stood on the next corner, one gloved hand on the handle of a walking stick. His topper was frayed but had clearly been fine once, as had his dusty coat and leather boots that now caved at the heels.

"Excuse me, sir," said Jack.

The man jumped. "I say!" he said, facing Jack.

Jack jumped, too, for the man's face was a terrific, terrible sight. It would have been quite normal were it not for the tiny brass grille set into his oversized nostrils. Jack had never seen such a thing. Tiny clasps held it to skin that was a sickly pale, and he had eyes like runny eggs.

"What are you staring at?" he demanded, adjusting his hold on his walking stick. Jack couldn't quite tell what the handle was, something made of cogs and hinges and bits of brass, half-concealed by a velvet glove that sagged, as if within it the hand were only bone.

"N-nothing, sir," said Jack. "I was just—"

"Lung complaint," snapped the man. "Don't goggle as if you've never seen such a thing."

"I'm sorry. That's a fine walking stick, sir. May I see it?"

The man didn't let it go, but moved his grip so's Jack could get a proper look. The handle was some kind of bird, wings formed of gears and spread so that a hand could rest between them. Its mouth was open in song. Jack had never seen anything like it.

"It's beautiful," he said.

"Hmmm." He peered at Jack, who could hear the air snorting through the grille, taking in his sodden clothes.

"Brave thing, being out in the rain. Youngsters don't have two thoughts to rub together."

"Could you point me to Mayfair?" Jack asked. "Please. If it's not too much trouble."

The top hat wobbled and slipped down. The runny eyes slid up and down the street from under the brim. "Mayfaer?" The man pronounced it oddly, but accents were twelve a penny. "You're a long way from home, lad. Unless that's not where you live?" He took in Jack's somewhat disheveled appearance. "Think there might be good pickings up there, do you?" Air wheezed in and out of the grille, the man's chest rising, falling, rising.

"No! I live there. *Sir*. That is, my parents do."

"Hmmm." He jabbed with his walking stick. "Thataway. 'Long the walk, y'see. You'll be wanting to head through the park—fastest way on foot. Turn at the birdcage. There's carriages round about, but I don't imagine a young ruffian such as yourself has any coin, do you?"

Jack's pockets were empty save for the compass. The morning at the outfitters with Mrs. Pond felt long ago, far away.

"Do you know the time?" Jack asked. The man tilted his strange face up, eyes squinting at the clock tower across the road. They looked as if they were being eaten by his face.

"Not a clue. Daft thing hasn't worked in weeks."

"Yes, it has." Jack stared at the man. Perhaps he was addled. "Sorry, sir. Thank you very much."

"You're very . . . pink," said the man.

There was nothing much to say to that, and the man was certainly addled. Jack left him standing there, still leaning on the stick, snorting through metal.

What an odd thing that was. The work of one of the Harley Street doctors, no doubt, though Jack wondered what kind of problem would cause them to do *that*.

Jack hurried, head down, watching his feet, and so he did not see. More clouds threatened on the horizon, but for the moment it was dry. Doors opened. From the corner of his eye, he caught one of the new motorcars pull to a stop at the curb, but there was no time to stop and admire it. He ran, leaving the gardens and the tower and the Palace of Westminster behind him, curious stares brushing over him, unnoticed as a breeze.

And so he did not see.

The road was wide, sweeping, overhung with spindly trees whose branches spat unwanted rain. Long, low buildings lined one side, and on the other, a sprawling park carpeted in limp, wet grass. None of it was especially familiar to Jack, but he thought he remembered which park it was, the splotch on a map his father kept.

Jack turned onto a path in sore need of repair, slabs chipped, their edges crumbling.

Ahead, just before the path curved out of sight, a gazebo sat raised above the lawns, and indeed it looked, from a distance, like an ornate birdcage.

Someone was inside it, her back to him, long hair pinned in elaborate curls. Jack hurried, boots slipping on the wet ground. She might give better directions than "Thataway."

"Excuse me, miss!" Good impressions were important. She would want to help this polite young man, soaked and cold, clearly eager to get home. "Excuse me," he said again, stepping closer when she appeared not to have heard him the first time.

Still, she did not turn. Raindrops bounced off the gilded cage in which she stood, dry beneath the domed brass roof. Beside it now, Jack found a small set of steps leading inside. "Hello?" he asked quietly, so as not to frighten her, but loud enough that she could hear him over the *thump-thump* of rain, which was louder than he'd expected, amplified by the metal.

Her face was smooth, eyes glassy, lashes long and curled. Like a doll, thought Jack, though he knew little of such things. Dolls were for girls, or so Father always said. Jack had his set of toy soldiers, but those weren't dolls; they

were an army. Certainly they didn't wear lace dresses or silly shoes or blue ribbons in their hair.

"Can you hear me?" Jack asked, wondering if there was something wrong with her that caused the strange, blank expression. Or perhaps all girls were like that. The only one Jack knew was his cousin Susan, who liked to poke him with sticks and run away.

The girl opened her mouth. "I . . . ," she began. Jack waited. "I . . . ," she said again. As he watched, the most curious thing happened: Her mouth closed, opened, and closed once more. Her arms dropped limply to her sides, and her eyelids slid down, shutting with a *click*, just before her head lolled to the front, those ribbons blowing in the wind.

"Are you ill?"

One of her fingers twitched. He stepped closer, unsure what he was supposed to do if she *was* ill. At school, the matron was sent for. At home, a doctor would come with a black leather bag full of steel and gauze.

Around the birdcage, the wind picked up, howling like a kicked dog. A gust blew, ruffling the girl's dress, making the ribbons shiver as her hair blew away from her neck to show the key hidden there.

Jack stared. He thought of the soldiers, lined up in rows on a shelf in his bedroom.

"Why," he whispered, "you're a windup girl, and not a real girl at all."

CHAPTER FIVE

The Lady's Anger

W HEN LORCAN ENTERED THE presence of the Lady, he did so proudly, his back straightened and shoulders squared by her trust. He had always been such a good son to her, a good servant.

His hands shook. He had wanted to resist the lure of the palace, his wish to return to her. The fleets needed inspecting, of course. War crept ever closer on the horizon, and the Empire of Clouds *would* triumph. He could sleep on his own dirigible as it sailed to the four corners of the island, a sooty jewel that was nonetheless the finest in the Empire's crown. Put the airships all in order, stationed as flags with their crimson sails and ready to set off at a word he would speak all too soon.

But he couldn't stay away from the palace, not now that he'd returned after such a long time gone. A confection, it was, a wedding cake of stone. No one spoke to him as he strode up the wide, low staircase, through the front doors, along the red carpet, down a corridor large enough to house a thousand weary men.

A tiny metal creature bounded up to his ankles. Lorcan considered kicking it, but there was no need; he would save his strength for later. "Meet me in the tower, Trinket," he said to the imp. It nodded and ran away much faster than it had come.

"Sir Lorcan has returned." A footman bowed low, straightened again with his back against the open door. An arm, lost in the Last Great Battle, the last war fought by the Empire before these many years of peace that were near an end, was brass to the elbow.

Lorcan stepped inside. The polished floor reflected his fine suit, his loud footsteps. The room was richer than a feast, gold and velvet and glass. Tiny silver faeries hovered around stuttering flames in their crystal bulbs, as faeries are wont to do. The light flickered and licked at their wings, and Lorcan patted his pockets.

"Where is he?"

This time, it was Lorcan who bowed.

"Lady," he said, standing straight once more. "You look well." Oh, she was always a vision in blue, that deep shade of almost-midnight, as if she had torn down the sky to wear as silk. He had no doubt she could do just that if she wished. Several ladies-in-waiting giggled, clustered around the throne. Her dark hair was in ringlets today, shot through with jewels, snaking from beneath a tiny top hat crowned with feathers.

"Flatterer," said the Lady with a smile.

A bowl of ripe apples with thin golden skins sat on a table beside her. For him, he knew. She was so kind, so thoughtful.

"Well, come closer, dearest, and tell me all about him. Is he upstairs? Have you already taken him to his room? Does he simply adore it? Of course he must, but I wish to meet him! Arabella!"

One of the young ladies rose, a chit of a thing with a face like soured milk. Fresh blooms sat in a vase on a table, and she moved toward them.

"Yes, Lady?"

"In the nursery, you will find the most perfect little boy. Not a hint of brass, not a gear in sight. Do fetch him and bring him to me."

"Yes, Lady," said Arabella.

Lorcan's choices weighed heavy. Tangible things, one

in each hand. Letting the girl go would give him another five minutes, perhaps more if her feet moved as slowly as her brain.

"Stay," he told her. She was nearly between himself and the Lady, and that was good. One step to the right . . .

Arabella blinked. So did the Lady. Only Lorcan knew what the slight thinning of those lips meant. Already she was considering ways to punish him for his insolence. Questioning her orders in front of another, why, that was simply not done.

"Do you wish to tell me something, Lorcan?" asked the Lady. She stood. Her shoes peeked from the hem of her gown. Heels clicked on the floor. "My dearest, you may tell me anything. You know this."

Her skin was perfumed with stars, her eyes hard as flint.

"There has been . . . There has been a setback, Lady," he said. "He was not right for you. Already I am looking for the perfect one, and he will be found, brought to you. I swear it."

The girls had ceased their giggling. Arabella stood, frozen, one foot turned toward the door. She could have reached out to touch both Lorcan and the Lady, but of course she did not.

For one brief, hovering moment, the room was a held breath, broken only by the steel-flutter of faery wings, for they did not know or care. Lorcan met the Lady's eyes.

And waited.

"I think," she said, a hint of pink tongue darting out between her lips. "I think you are lying to me. Did you fail, Lorcan, dearest? Were you outwitted by a child? Or perhaps, perhaps you did not want to bring me my new son. Tell me why you are lying."

He stepped backward. A mistake. That damnable fool of a mother had ruined *everything*. "I would never dare to do such a thing, Lady."

The Lady's head tilted, and a gloved hand reached as if to strike him, but it did not. Instead, the softest satin brushed gently over Lorcan's cheek. "You were so young, once," she mused. "So young and so innocent. You would sit at my feet and play with the automatons the metallurgists would make for you. You loved me then."

A faery, perhaps blinded by the glow, flew into the lantern glass, and it rang through the room like a bell. "As I do still, Mother."

He knew at once. The silly girls knew. Even the faeries seemed to know, for their wings stopped fluttering and they landed on the edges of things with soft *clunks*.

The Lady's mouth twisted. Sparks rained from her eyes to land, sizzling, on her dress. "You *dare*!" she screamed. "You dare call me that? YOU DARE, EVEN AS YOU LIE TO ME?"

The force of her blow snapped his neck back. She could not harm him, not badly, but she could make him wish he were dead.

He did wish it. One of her rings had caught him, and he felt the blood flow, burning, fiery, and turn to dry ash on his cheek. The girls stared, wordless, confused. One let out a nervous giggle.

The Lady waved her hand. The girl fell to the floor without time even for a final breath, a grimace frozen on her face.

In a swirl of midnight, the Lady stormed across the room. The faeries flew for cover, tucking themselves behind books on the shelves, flying up to perch on the great gas chandelier. Crystal shattered, skittering in razor-sharp diamonds across the floor. A priceless vase smashed to shards.

"I will fix it, Lady," Lorcan said, loud over the curtains tearing. Light fell reluctantly into the room. The ladies-in-waiting, seizing their chance, ran from it, nearly bowling over the footman in their haste, leaving the dead one behind. "I will find you another. A better son."

An apple missed him by an inch, slamming into a Tune-Turner behind. The enormous cone wobbled and fell with a deafening crash.

"I want the one I was promised. Why, the artist has already begun his portrait, but he can do only so much from a mere photograph. We must see the boy, and I have suffered this foolishness long enough, Lorcan. Do you hear me? I do not want cats or butterflies or girls who must be wound up every morning! Do your duty, as all those who came before you did, and bring. Me. My. Son."

Lorcan raised his chin. "He will be yours."

"See to it. Oh and, Lorcan? I do think it's time you called me Andrasta."

So she was his mother no more. Lorcan bowed, stiffly, in place of speech. He would get the boy and she would forgive him. He would be her most trusted once again.

Oh, yes.

CHAPTER SIX

The Windup Girl

A WINDUP GIRL. WHOEVER HEARD of such a thing?

"You *look* real," he said to her. Once, Mrs. Pond had taken him to a circus, where a pair of puppeteers had performed an elaborate act with marionettes on strings. The puppets' faces had been shiny, wooden, plump lips painted a too-bright pink, eyes too wide, and even those were enough to haunt Jack's dreams for weeks.

This girl had no strings.

Her eyes, though closed—he remembered the *click*—were lashed with what he was certain was real hair. Her fingers curled like proper hands. Jack bent down. Tiny hinges made knuckles below neatly trimmed fingernails.

Or rather, formed, because these would never grow. She had been built. In a workshop somewhere, perhaps. There would be a little box of teeth, another, larger, of eyeballs, drawers full of rivets and wires and long trunks of copper pipes for bones.

He poked her, pulled his finger away as if burned.

Experimentally, Jack touched his own arm, watched the flesh dent beneath and pop back into shape when he took his hand away.

He poked her again. Her . . . skin, for he could not think of a better word despite knowing a great many words, stayed smooth as a wall, a china plate.

That was *extremely* odd.

The key at her neck was shaped like a butterfly's wing, with two large holes punched through the brass at the top and bottom. The edges dug into Jack's thumb and forefinger as he gripped it.

Winding her up mustn't be so very wrong, not if she was meant to be so. And there was no soul about to tell him off for messing with things as didn't belong to him.

Slowly, he turned the key.

Nothing happened, not at first. One spin, two, three. He braced his feet on the soft wooden floorboards of the cage, cold toes curled inside wet socks. Seven, eight, nine.

On the tenth, her eyes snapped open, whizzing blue in

their sockets. Jack hopped back again, nearly tripping in his haste to get away from her suddenly, as if it hadn't been him who'd brought her to life.

"Hello," she said, voice just like a girl's. Her lips moved, stiffly but no more so than Mother's when she was talking to someone to whom she must be polite.

"You can talk," said Jack.

"Hello." She looked at him.

"Can you say anything else?"

"'Course I can. Can you?"

"Um," said Jack. There were a thousand things he wanted to ask, just like at school when they were learning something interesting and the teachers kept the really good bits to themselves so Jack and his classmates would raise their hands. But there was no one else here, and Jack's hands were by his sides, held there so he wouldn't poke her again. That seemed wrong now. "I'm Jack. Do you have a name?"

"Hello"—she blinked, looking for all the world and people in it as if she were thinking—"Jack. I'm Beth. Beth Number Thirteen."

Jack thought about this for a moment. "There are twelve more of you?"

"Somewhere. You're very pink. And a little bit stupid."

"That's not very nice," snapped Jack.

"I'm not very nice." Beth folded her hands together. "But Dr. Snailwater says I am supposed to try. I'm sorry," she said, not sounding particularly sorry at all.

"All right." *Very pink.* She was the second person to say that.

"Were you trying to stay out of the rain, too? You didn't do a very good job. You're all wet, so perhaps you *are* stupid. *Dry as a bone, no rust be known,*" Beth singsonged.

"But I don't rust in the rain." A feeling of having eaten too many jellied eels curled itself in Jack's belly, all squirm and slime. The empty streets.

"Don't you? Gosh. Are all your metal parts on the inside, then?"

"I haven't got any metal parts." How very cold and wet he was came back to Jack with a *whoosh.* Cold and wet and Mrs. Pond was going to be so angry. "I was trying to get home, to Mayfair."

Thunder rumbled. The birdcage shook. Beyond the park and lower than the sky, clouds gathered, a thick, swirling gray.

"You'll want to be going that way, then," said Beth, pointing. "'Round the lake. North." It was the most human she'd seemed so far, her eyes half-closed, mouth pressed together, and she looked away to stare across the park. "Oh, look. The airships are flying."

Jack followed her hand out to the horizon.

Not thunder at all. A tingle ran down his spine.

Brass grilles and clockwork girls and boats, boats sailing on the sky, great sheets hung from masts and holes for cannon fire.

"What . . . What are they?" he asked, not sure how he'd come to be sitting, knees pulled to his chest, the iron cage bars cold stripes at his back, as if another few steps would make the difference.

"The airships," Beth said again.

They were coming closer.

Jack knew, the way folks might know a dream they couldn't quite remember. Fuzzy on the surface, but the truth was there, deep down, running away from his efforts to grasp it.

And yet, at the same time, he didn't know at all.

He trudged through the park beneath the dull, swishy roar of the airships, Beth at his side.

She walked like a normal person, a normal person who'd been kicked in the knee. Every other step was a funny little skip, but it hadn't stopped her from insisting she come along so's he wouldn't get lost.

He didn't want to say anything to her, not until he was certain. Already she thought he was stupid. Pink and stupid.

Jack kicked a pebble. At least he wasn't a *toy*.

Overhead, the ships split the sky apart. Three of them, all in a row, beasts coughing out huge lungfuls of black smoke from enormous bellies. The smoke curled to streamers, like crepe paper for mourning, and then dissolved, lost forever to the clouds. Craning, squinting, Jack saw the lines where one plank met the next, thinking they must've taken an entire forest's worth of trees.

"To Mayfaer!" shouted Beth, skipping again. "Mayfaer and the Mayfaeries!"

Twenty minutes they walked, past the lake, through one park, across the avenue into the next. Beth kept carefully to the path, away from the grass still wet from the storm. So did Jack, his socks already quite wet enough. It was much faster this way, unhindered by the crush of carts and carriages that he'd been trapped in with Wilson and Mrs. Pond.

At Piccadilly—though whoever had written the street sign couldn't spell, as it said PICK-A-DILLY, just like that—they stopped.

Or rather, Jack did. For the streets were not empty now.

Hulking motorcars slid through their own clouds of steam, the windows darkened so he couldn't see inside. People bustled, all of them a curious mix of flesh and metal. A grille, a hand, a strange, deep *clank* when a few gasped and shied from Jack. Goggles to protect against the new fog of soot, gathering again after the rain. A foot falling far too heavy within its shoe, *thunk*ing against greasy cobbles.

This was where Mr. Havelock had come. Not *here,* possibly, but here. This place.

Something half as high as Jack's knee poked him hard in the shin with a steel finger and ran away, cackling.

"Ow!"

Beth stopped, turned, a smile on her pretty doll's face.

"What is *that?*" Jack demanded, rubbing his leg, staring down the street at the thing. Wings, it had, wings of steel and copper and oh, that was very strange, indeed.

She didn't seem to think he was getting any cleverer. "Just a Mis-Chief, silly goose. Commanders of the Order of Daft, assistants to the Guild of Giddiness. It's a sort of faery."

The imaginary eels in Jack's belly stirred and began to swim.

It looked just like a very ordinary street. Like Piccadilly. Like . . . London. Shops and merchants and people complaining about the price of things as they parted with their coins.

But at the same time, it did not. It was true he did not know London well, but he was sure nonetheless that none of the shops there had an enormous copper dragon scale behind the plate glass, guaranteed lucky.

And there weren't these clouds of soot falling low, folding themselves around everything they touched. Not like this. Not so very black and choking, billowing from the steam carriages, the motorcars, every chimney Jack could see if he squinted.

"Hurry," Jack said, grasping Beth's arm. They dodged across the road. From there it was only a short walk to where, in another place, Jack's home sat.

He knew it wouldn't be here. Knew before he saw the great, looming factory taking up the entire stretch of road where there should be neat houses, doorsteps freshly limed and gleaming. Mrs. Pond and her counterparts should be in humid kitchens while ladies took tea in velvet parlors.

No kitchens or parlors hid behind these walls. The ground shook. A rumble churned through the air, and huge mists plumed from gratings in the ground, turning Beth the fake girl into a real ghost, a hazy gray shape.

"There you go," Beth said. "Don't see what's so special about it, why you were in such a rush to come here, but go inside if you must. Sure the foreman will box your ears for you at being gone."

Jack shook his head. "I used to . . . This was my house."

"Don't look much like anybody's house to me."

"No," Jack agreed.

"Where would you like to go next, then?"

"Er."

Beth began to wander away, back in the direction of the busy street, so that Jack had to trot to catch up with her. "I came in through the clock," he said, which didn't make much sense when he said it out loud, but she didn't appear to be listening anyway. And Jack didn't want to go back to the clock, not just yet.

He supposed he should find Mr. Havelock at some point, if this churning, industrious place hadn't swallowed him up whole, never to be seen again.

Mr. Havelock truly was a magician, and such a thing was even easier to believe here than it had been when Jack watched the flower die and come back to life, or the hairpin fly. Another faery scuttled by, pulling bootlaces loose on all the feet it passed.

"Anywhere," Jack said to Beth. "Take me anywhere. I want to see everything."

"I like you," said Beth. "Right then! Adventure!"

"Are there just faeries here?" Jack asked as Beth turned the corner, ducking and dodging among the people. "Are they all made of metal? Is *everyone*?"

Beth shook her head, calling over her shoulder about dragons and unicorns as she led him to a wide, open square packed with market stalls. "There's a hundred kinds of faery, and they're all right scamps. Lots of the other creatures is mechanical, too," she said, "'cept for those folks eat cows and suchlike. And me, I'm mechanical, but I'm a bit special. Mostly people are like you, but with metal parts where's they need them."

And they needed them to breathe. Jack thought of the grille in the old man's nose. Already his own chest was aching from running through the soupy gray air, but that was small concern compared to what was in front of him. The market was a riot of color, bright against dull brick and all the pale people doing their shopping. Jack spied the normal sorts of things—pies and cheeses—and plenty so abnormal he couldn't begin to name them. One sold great woven tapestries showing a golden bird, the same as he'd seen on the walking stick, but that made sense now, if the birds here were metal, not bone. There were tables of strange clockwork devices, bowls of herbs he'd never seen in the garden at home, and an old woman telling fortunes she read in a pool of oil.

"How'd you come in through the clock?" Beth asked, pulling him from the market and down into an alley thin as a hair. "Not saying I believe you, but you are properly odd, and I like a good story much as anyone."

She had already said he was too pink. Jack felt himself

go slightly pinker. "Well, see, I followed someone. A magician who had come to my home and wanted to take me away with him." Mr. Havelock had wanted to bring Jack *here*, and for a moment Jack hated his mother afresh. He could have seen this days ago, and she'd stopped it. "I should find him, I think."

"Oh." Beth smiled. "That's easy enough, if you'll just tell me his name. I knows everyone from all my wandering. Drives the doctor mad. Who is this magician?"

"His name is Mr. Havelock," Jack answered, thinking very hard. "Mr. *Lorcan* Havelock."

Beth was pale, built that way, Jack was certain, and just as sure that she would have gone paler at the name if it were possible.

"But he's a horrible man," she said slowly, backing a few steps away from Jack on the cramped, cobbled street. "An evil, horrible man, and you don't seem horrible. What'd you want him for?"

No. That couldn't be. Mr. Havelock had been kind and polite and clever. He had wanted to teach Jack magic.

The same magic, perhaps, that made his eyes glow red as the devil's in the parlor lamplight. The same that made the flower die at his touch.

"You're not so pink now," she said, as Jack's knees knocked together. "I think we should see Dr. Snailwater.

Best doctor in all of Londinium. Fix anything, he will."

Londinium. Jack thought he must look afraid, but he wasn't. He was far from home, surrounded by magic and clockwork, and surely this windup girl was wrong about Mr. Havelock.

This was *brilliant.*

CHAPTER SEVEN
Crystal & Copper

H E HAD BEEN RIGHT ABOUT the boxes of teeth. All laid out in rows on a long table, neat as chessmen.

It had taken nearly an hour to turn their backs on the market and walk through the streets Jack had seen from carriage windows with Mrs. Pond that morning.

Now that felt days before, and the streets were all different. He kept stopping to gape, fishlike, at more metal faeries, more people who were not entirely flesh and blood, but who smiled and shopped and worried as if they were. At the stinking, oily slime that coated the sky and everything below.

And now they were here. Even Jack, back home, had

heard of Harley Street. But here there was another *e*, to make it Harleye Street. He'd even come once when he'd taken ill and a white-coated man couldn't pay a visit to the house. Beth had walked smartly up to a door like any other, set into dirty brown brick, windows either side hung red with curtains.

"Come in. Come in," said the shaggy man who must be Dr. Snailwater. He looked like an old suit, wrinkled, frayed, and lumpy from mothballs, but his hair was a shock of white fluff, like a dandelion.

Shelves lined the walls, sagging under the weight of slimy things in jars. Strange machines dotted the floor, sat atop rickety benches. Steam hissed slowly from one in a far corner, creating a miasma of cloud at the ceiling, and the bloody tang of copper came at Jack from every direction.

"Well, well," said Dr. Snailwater, walking in a circle around Beth. He lifted her fingers to inspect the hinges, bending them one by one. Beth stood perfectly still. He held open her eyelids, peering in, squinting himself until he nodded in satisfaction. "Some of my best work, you." He crouched down and picked up her foot so her leg bent at the knee. "Not good enough though. Bit creaky, eh? You, boy, fetch that turnscrew."

It wasn't much of a help. Tools of all sizes littered every

surface not used by something else, but Dr. Snailwater waved a hand in the general direction and, after a few false starts, Jack found the right one.

Much as Jack wanted to watch, the moment Dr. Snailwater peeled Beth's skin from a hidden seam at the joint, Jack turned, carefully fixing his eyes on what looked like a linen press, for taking the wrinkles from clothing, crossed with an octopus. If an octopus could be fashioned from steel.

The sound of the screws tightening was bad enough. Jack flinched at every click, but Beth was silent, and Jack took it from this that Dr. Snailwater wasn't hurting her.

"Better," said Dr. Snailwater, his own knees snapping as he stood. "And all wound up, too? Excellent."

"I did that," said Jack.

"Yes, and who might you be? Doesn't take a genius to see that you're an odd one, and I *am* a genius. From the country, are we? I'd say the mountains, but you don't speak like one, and I know voices, lad. They're a job to get right, I can say."

"I'm Jack. Jack Foster."

"Dr. Mephisto Snailwater. A pleasure. For you, naturally."

"I think he's lost," Beth mused, inspecting a crimson marble she'd found on one of the many tables. "And he says he doesn't have any metal on him. Not inside, neither. And he knows Sir Lorcan."

"I see. Is he a *friend* of Sir Lorcan's?"

"Not exactly," said Jack. The doctor's expression told him this was the correct answer.

"Well, now. Lost? Youngsters knew how to read maps in my day." He shook his head. "There's one 'round here somewhere."

"How do you do it?" Jack gazed around again at the boxes and bottles and jars. "You make *people* in here."

The doctor's eyes lit up. "I try. I try."

"But how?"

"Aha," said Dr. Snailwater. "It's all in the measurements, you see." Darting across the room, he plucked an eyeball from a glass bowl. "Bit under an inch. Good for your old lady who peers out through the curtains. Beady, you know. And here!"—he dug in a drawer, held up a fully formed hand cut off at the wrist—"nice and strong. Sturdy fingers. This one's for the shipyards, I fear. Repairs every week after."

Jack stared. The fingernails were dirty.

"Do you build everything?" Jack thought of the faery who had poked him in the shin, and said so.

Dr. Snailwater chuckled. "Magical creatures are a bit beyond my specialty, I'm afraid. The gods built the first ones. Now they build each other. I study them, o' course. Much to learn, much to learn."

"And t-those?" he asked, pointing at the jars.

Dr. Snailwater's face creased into a frown. "Always trying to perfect my art," he said, shuffling over to pick one up. Something sloshed in the liquid inside. "Liver. Eight inches. Going to have a terrible sense of humor, this one, if I ever manage it. Not funny at all." He hoisted another. "Spleen. Good for a temper, see."

Jack didn't know whether to be revolted or fascinated. He opened his mouth, caught the boxes of teeth from the corner of his eye, and closed it again. It was just dawning on him that, to a man who kept livers in jars, Jack himself was a collection of neatly packaged parts.

Dr. Snailwater laughed again. "You're safe here, boy. I see you have many questions. The shape of your nostrils. Curious, yet willing to accept the strange. Upstairs with you, and I'll answer the ones I can. Beth knows the way."

She moved behind him, and Jack started. He'd almost forgotten she was there, that she'd brought him to this house. It was clear she was familiar with it, in the way she slid easily between tables and stepped over things on the floor. At the back of the room, a door led to a narrow, winding staircase, the carpet threadbare, coming loose in spots. Jack held the banister so as not to trip, but Beth swung her arms at her sides, and her walk was smoother than before.

The sitting room was as cluttered as the workshop. Binoculars of all shapes and sizes filled a glass case; a dozen pocket watches on the mantel told different times. A tiny model train chugged on a winding track overhead. In the middle of a round table by the window, a crystal ball sat on brass legs atop a faded black velvet tablecloth. These, Jack knew of. His mother's spiritualist—before Mr. Havelock—had brought one, and the door to the parlor was always closed, the curtains drawn, a few moments after she arrived and took it from her bag.

"It won't help you," said Dr. Snailwater, ambling into the room in time to catch Jack with his nose almost touching it. "Tetchy thing. Only sees the past, which is frankly useless to a forward thinker such as myself. I keep it as a paperweight." He set a mug of black tea down in front of Jack, muttering about always forgetting milk. "Now, tell me what's going on."

Jack looked at Beth, swinging her legs from a highbacked armchair. At the little train, which had paused beside a stretch of bookshelf to take on a group of tiny passengers clustered there.

"There's nothing that would surprise me, lad. Speak up."

"I want to know where I am," Jack said.

"Now, that," answered the doctor, "is a most interesting thing to say."

In the darkness, Jack rolled over on the pallet of blankets Dr. Snailwater had made up for him on the floor. Fusty, crumbling, scented with the powdery death of a thousand insects.

Beth sat in a chair, fingers curled over the arms. She wasn't asleep. She wasn't . . . anything. This time, Jack wasn't tempted to wind her up again. Not yet, in the still and the silence where he could think.

The Empire of Clouds. It made sense. The swirling fog of steam, soot, and filth had hung over the land as long as almost anyone could remember and, Dr. Snailwater said, cleared for only a few minutes after each of the frequent storms.

And the people, the faeries, the creatures would run for cover when the rains came. *Dry as a bone, no rust be known*, that's what Beth had said in the birdcage. Because of the metal, and it was this, this that made Jack's heart race.

A land of brass and steel and clockwork, of steam and airships, cogs that turned and wheels that spun. He half wondered if he was dreaming, so perfect was this place, and would wake in his bed to the sound of Mrs. Pond clattering the breakfast things in the kitchen below.

Jack felt a bit sick. Mrs. Pond would miss him. But his mother would probably be glad for him to stay here forever, and he thought he just might do exactly such. That would show them.

On the other side of the room, the crystal ball glowed in the moonlight.

It couldn't hurt to *look*.

The blankets crackled under his knees; too-large socks slipped on his feet. Dr. Snailwater had put Jack's clothes in a machine the size of a motorcar, and for several minutes Jack watched his filthy clothes froth in the water like angry sea serpents devouring a fish.

He crept to the table. Beyond the window, out on the street, silvery things the size of birds but were most assuredly not birds did a sort of elegant dance in the glow of a gas lamp, wings fluttering, flashing. Jack watched until the unheard music in their heads stopped and they lit on the lamppost.

Against the black velvet cloth that looked not so dusty in the dark, the crystal ball was a perfect moon, shining, suspended, ethereal. Close enough to touch and somehow too far away, too.

It did not occur to Jack that he wouldn't be able to make it work. Time after time he'd knelt at the keyhole. There was nothing particularly special to do, no need to turn around three times or say a special prayer to the dead. Just a simple matter of concentration.

The table creaked. The velvet whispered. "Show me," he said, which was unnecessary, but it felt as if there should be *something*.

Inside the ball, the mist shivered. Jack breathed deeply, leaning closer. A cloud skimmed the surface and cleared again almost at once.

"Show me," he said again, louder. Too loud. Had Beth been able to hear him, he would certainly have awoken her. He saw his own reflection, bloated around the ball's smooth curve.

Within, the milky glow began to thin, darken, ripple, and spread. Heat washed over Jack's hands; he touched the crystal and immediately pulled back, sucking his finger to soothe the burn.

The mist cleared, and there he was. Not his reflection, but him. The orb was the eye of a bird, looking down from the rafters of a train station at Jack, still in his school clothes, and Mother in her pretty green dress. Other passengers blurred unimportantly at the edges.

Mr. Havelock stood, perfectly clear, suit sharp as knives. Clearly, he was waiting.

Waiting.

Mother stepped away to see to Jack's trunk.

Waiting for Jack.

It was clear, clearer than the crystal ball into which Jack gazed. Mr. Havelock stood aside, watched as Jack and his mother fetched his things, followed them out to the hansom that would take them to Mayfair. And he followed.

He'd ventured from the Empire of Clouds to the London Jack knew for Jack himself. This much, Jack knew already, but he hadn't known Mr. Havelock was watching him so closely. Why, though? To teach Jack his magician's secrets? What made Jack special?

You heard stories, Jack thought. Stories of evil men, of bloodied corpses left to rot. They came even to him, from

Wilson to the gardener to Mrs. Pond, to Jack listening at the keyhole. Where Wilson heard them, Jack didn't know, but they slithered through the house in hushed voices until everyone knew.

Jack trembled. His eyes closed, and when he opened them again, he was in the cab, the horses snorting.

The mist in the ball darkened and closed. Jack pulled back, dizzied, confused. A thrill shot through him.

He was supposed to be here. This city of steam, this Empire of Clouds, wanted him, where none in his own London noticed or cared if he was there or not. Sending him off to school. Tucking him away in the kitchen or his bedchamber while parties tinkled in the dining room.

He almost missed it, so deep was he in thought. The mist flickered again.

And then it shook, so violently the crystal ball itself rattled on its silver stand, and from the parting gray something burst, copper and brass and silent screams from a pointed mouth.

A beak.

At him it flew, closer and closer until its eyes swallowed the orb, huge, golden eyes full of fire and rage, and the ball broke apart in large, jagged chunks that smashed the windows, sent Jack flying backward.

"Foolish boy!"

He was on the floor. His head pounded. Over him leaned the nightshirted figure of Dr. Snailwater. The blue stripes of the cloth wiggled, making Jack's head ache.

"There, now, you're quite all right," said the doctor, and he was a doctor so he should know. "Did no one ever teach you not to touch what's not yours?"

"I broke it," whispered Jack, his stomach tying itself into a neat row of knots. "I'm sorry! I'll find you another. I'll—"

"It is perfectly fine," said Dr. Snailwater, and it was. There, on its stand, floating above the black velvet, the crystal ball was a full moon again. Jack's head pounded harder.

"I don't understand."

Dr. Snailwater was busy measuring the distance between Jack's eyebrows. "Quite. But rest assured, it would take more than a titchy fingersmith like yourself to destroy it. You'd best be sitting and telling me what you saw." The doctor stood and moved to the chair where Beth sat, a thing but a girl too. The turning of the key filled the room. Her eyes opened and her neck twisted so she could smile at Dr. Snailwater, then frown at the darkness.

"Your friend thought it mightn't be a bad idea to poke his little pink nose into affairs that don't concern him," he explained.

"I saw myself in it," said Jack.

Beth and Dr. Snailwater turned slowly to look at him.

"Before it smashed, I mean." It was all a bit fuzzy, like the blurred passengers.

He told them.

Beth sat very rigid. Her key wound down.

"That explains a great deal," said the doctor, returning with another pot of his thick tea.

"Why was he looking for me?" asked Jack, expecting Dr. Snailwater, who seemed to know a great deal about everything, to answer. But it was Beth who spoke.

"The Lady," was all she said.

"Indeed," the doctor agreed.

Jack looked from one to the other. He didn't like this, that things were being kept from him. He was special, after all. Hadn't he come through the door? Didn't he deserve an answer? "Tell me," he said, and it was not a request.

"Big for your britches, aren't you?" huffed Dr. Snailwater. He waved his hand, the tea sloshing like a black ocean in a cup. "All right. All right. A place can't be without someone to boss it about. You've got someone in your world, yes?"

"Too many, Father says." The queen was old and gray, always dressed in mourning clothes for her husband, who had died long before Jack was born—before even his parents were born—but there were others besides. Dukes and duchesses, lords and ladies, enough politicians to fill Westminster.

Dr. Snailwater nodded. "Well, we've got the Lady. Been around long as anyone can remember. And Sir Lorcan, too. There's lords and duchesses and such in the colonies, though for how much longer they'll be the colonies is anyone's guess. Here, we've got the Lady and Sir Lorcan."

"They must be very old," said Jack.

"Wouldn't know it to look at them," said Beth. "They say *he* made a deal with the faeries so's he'd never grow old. Sir Lorcan is the Lady's son, but the Lady likes children she can coddle and stuff with sweets. And she never lets you out, or takes you anywhere, and it's very boring, but I liked her."

"All mothers are like that," he said. He wondered if she missed him. If she was frantic with worry, she and his father pounding their fists on the counter at Scotland Yard. *He's just a little boy,* they'd say.

Dr. Snailwater laughed humorlessly. "Perhaps."

"I don't understand. Why does she need to steal children from . . . from *my* London? Why does she not have one of her own, or—" *Or steal one from here*, he wished to say, but it was a buzzing wasp of a thought, cruel inside his throbbing head.

"The Lady is not like us, not like any of us," said Dr. Snailwater. "No one knows from whence she came. It seems she is no longer satisfied with children like Beth."

"She likes pretty things," said Beth. Her eyelids clicked. "Pretty, perfect things. Flesh and blood, with no metal parts. There's lots of children here, but none like that."

Jack thought of the very first person he'd encountered here. And of the people on the streets, with their metal coughs. Dr. Snailwater's hand clinked against the china. Beth's skin wasn't really skin at all.

Oh.

"You understand."

Jack nodded at Dr. Snailwater, though he didn't understand, not everything. "You were hers," he said to Beth, who did not answer.

"Thirteen, I made. Each better than the last. Beth the best of all. Why, to look at her, you'd think she was entirely human. But not good enough, not good enough. Hearts are tricky things, you know. Take all the measurements you like, still impossible to get right. Cast her out with nothing. Folks wind her up as and when. She can come here to get out of the rain if she likes. The Lady's up to no good, and that rake Lorcan is worse."

So the Lady had been given children, but they hadn't loved her, and so Lorcan, who Jack had known as Mr.

Havelock, had come to steal Jack away. Jack pressed his hands to his eyes.

Dr. Snailwater pushed himself slowly from his chair, gathering cups, hanging their handles from his strange fingers. "If Lorcan could get to this London of yours, there's a way back through. Off to sleep with you, and tomorrow we'll find it."

"Why, though?" Jack asked the following morning. Dr. Snailwater looked at him over the top of an oozing boiled egg. "Why must I go home?"

The doctor considered this. "Your mother and father will be missing you, surely?"

Jack was not entirely convinced. "It's interesting here. London is boring, and I want to learn about all the clockwork and things. I'm good with that sort of stuff."

The egg sucked gloopily at the spoon. It wobbled as the doctor raised it to his mouth. "Interesting comes at a price, dear boy. You cannot fathom what you are asking."

"Then tell me," said Jack in a tone that would have earned him a hiding from Mrs. Pond, but got only a raised, bushy eyebrow from Dr. Snailwater.

"The glory of the Empire of Clouds," he said, almost to himself. "Look around you, lad. Do you want to end up as one of us?" He raised his metal hand. "Lives lost, sickness, for the privilege of industry. I must put new lungs into infants before they might draw their first breath. Give them eyes so they can see."

Better than a wig and a robe, thought Jack, *or an office among stacks of paper, choking with dust and sums.* But he did not say so. Something told him Dr. Snailwater wouldn't agree.

"There is no hope in Londinium, nor in all of the Empire. Even the fanciful comforts people once invented to give them solace have been forgotten, not that *it* ever existed at all. It is not safe for you here. You are as much of a curiosity to us as our faeries and clockwork birds must be to you. And if Sir Lorcan discovers that you followed him, well, I should say that's a thing we don't want to happen."

"I'll be careful," said Jack, thinking of the motorcars turning sharp corners, the evil-looking machine in the room below that would bite off a finger without hesitation.

"If only it were that simple—"

"If only what were that simple?" Beth asked, skipping into the room.

"Now, dear, we've talked about interrupting. Your friend here wishes to stay."

Beth turned her strange, seeing glass eyes to Jack. "Oh, yes!"

"No." The doctor's voice was firm. "I've things to see to. Go amuse yourselves, the pair of you, and leave the crystal ball alone."

Jack still hadn't told either of them about the thing inside the ball that made it break. It felt like his alone, somehow, if indeed he hadn't imagined it entirely. And in any case, it made him feel better to have a secret, certain as he was that Dr. Snailwater and Beth were still not telling him everything.

Beth showed him how to direct the tiny people on and off the train and to control the engine by means of an odd box with buttons that glowed when pressed. Together they made it stop at every bookshelf, alongside one of the bars of the chandelier, and trapped it in a tunnel set into the wall until they heard tiny, tinny screams from within.

They could not *make* him leave.

The bird in the ball was not Jack's only secret. For he had told Beth and Dr. Snailwater of following Lorcan through the door, but not precisely how he had come to do so. Not that the man had waited, eyes hidden behind his dark spectacles, for the clock in its famous tower to chime precisely twelve o'clock. That it might be just as simple to get home again.

Another clock, cloaked in a bell of pink glass, stood

on the mantel. Jack waited, pushed buttons with Beth, watched the little people with their satchels and shopping dart around thick, leather-bound tomes that would surely crush them if they were to tip over. The hands, needle-sharp, slowly swept the morning away.

CHAPTER EIGHT

A Simple Request

WHEN LORCAN RETURNED to the doorway, he did not need to wait for the chime of the bells. Not on this side, and in any case, they would not come. This side required a different trick. Heavy-pocketed, impatient, he stepped into the dark room, waited a breath, and stepped out again.

The light burned his eyes. Damnable people, with their electric lights and bright colors and the sun, oh, the sun most of all, without so much smoke and steam and soot to smother it. But the spectacles, slipped on, helped. Made it bearable.

He scarcely remembered the great fire here. He had been so young, and it was such a long time ago, but surely it was as bright as this when it tore through the hovel where Lorcan was born. He *did* remember the shiny golden coin, like a tiny flame itself, that had been his price, slipped into the grime-stained palm of a woman whose face Lorcan could no longer recall. Six hungry mouths had cried with wanting since the fire raged, and if the nice young man wanted to take one of them off her overworked hands, well, that was a blessing. It was over in moments, the exchange of coin and boy, and soon he was in a grand room in a grand palace with the grandest of ladies.

The Lady. That was where his memories truly began, and so he would do anything for her. What the Lady wanted, she would get, and she wanted this new son. The boy would still be at home, not yet returned to the school in the North.

Outside the gates of the Palace of Westminster, a score of hansoms waited for generous fares from the purses of pithy lords.

Such a pretty city. It was a shame about the people, the light. But he directed the Lady's architects to copy the bits he liked. It amused her to rule over her own London, the way she always should have. Two centuries before, Londinium had been a mess, a jumble of shacks cobbled together by the descendants of the first people to live there. Only the palace had been beautiful, though this, too, Lorcan had changed over the years.

To Mayfair, then, in the musty cab, above the cesspit of pickpockets and urchins, muck and mundanity.

The boy's street was quiet, but for a few carriages clustered outside his home. The fool was evidently entertaining again, but no matter. Indeed, this might be all to the good. She might not be so quick to refuse him a second time, not in front of her silly guests.

And if she did, well, he had other ways.

The chit of a maid answered the bell, apron creased, petticoats crusted with dirt.

"Mr. Lorcan Havelock, for Mrs. Foster." So polite. So careful.

For the moment.

"Madam isn't"—the girl sniffled, possibly under the weather—"receiving today, sir."

Lorcan frowned, quick as winking. "My business is, indeed, with young Master Jack. Would he be about?"

The girl goggled. A crumpled handkerchief peeked from her fist. "Jack?" she whispered. "But he's missing, sir, gone since yesterday, and Mrs. Pond 'as been dismissed for not mindin' 'im close enough! And we've had all the coppers 'round, all last night and into the dawn, but he's nowhere! How can a boy be nowhere?"

Gone. But it couldn't be.

"I *must* see Mrs. Foster," Lorcan insisted, dry

mouthed. "I can assist." Such a smooth lie. Nearly.

The girl simply would not move, but she was a tiny thing. Lorcan pushed past, onto the checkerboard floor. The parlor door stood ajar, letting through a rustle of whispers and tears.

"YOU! What have you done with my son?" screamed the fool the moment Lorcan stepped inside. He lacked normal blood in his veins, certainly it would never run cold, but he imagined it there, turning to ice.

"Pardon me?" he asked quite cautiously.

"What is the meaning of this?" demanded a man, bearded and portly, rising from a chair beside her. Lorcan removed his glasses, unnecessary with the drawn curtains, the low lamps. Mrs. Foster's eyes were red-rimmed, her hair falling from its pins.

"You asked me for him! What have you done with him?"

"I did not take young Jack," Lorcan said. A very careful truth. "I do not know where in this great city he is. You have my word."

The fool deflated as if pricked with a pin. "This is Mr. Havelock, Wallace, darling," she said quietly. "Of the Spiritualist Society. But what he is doing here, I'm sure I couldn't say. We had no appointment."

"Then I will thank him to leave," said her husband. The boy's father. Months and months, and Lorcan had barely caught glimpses of him, stepping from the house to the carriage before the sun woke, returning for a supper by light of candles and diamonds. "Jack is missing. There's no time for your nonsense."

A fresh wave of tears slicked the fool's face. But Lorcan felt no pity. There was no room for it, what with all the hope suddenly welling inside him.

If he could only find the boy first, before the constables, before he came home of his own accord, weary of adventure. These people would never know he *could* have been found. The grief now was at its very worst. It would get better with age, as so many things did.

"In fact," said Lorcan, not moving an inch on the rug, "I do believe this is precisely the time. Your good wife can attest to my skills as a spiritualist." Parlor tricks, all, but perhaps not such a very great waste of time now. "We have ways, you see, that policemen do not."

"Tosh!" said Wallace Foster, turning his back, but the fool sat straighter in her chair.

"You can find him?"

"Perhaps. Perhaps." Oh, yes. The Lady would get what she desired, and she would be happy and smiling. She would clap her hands and give him apples and all would be right in Londinium, even if this city crumbled to dust. "But I will require something."

"Anything, anything you need."

Wallace Foster snorted, but he said not a word. Lorcan told her, and the maid was summoned.

Moments later, he had it, held between thumb and forefinger. A wisp. Almost nothing, but the girl had freshened the beds and cleaned the combs at Mrs. Pond's direction while she and Jack went to the outfitters.

A single hair. Enough, with any luck.

CHAPTER NINE

The Man with Half a Face

W E SHALL HAVE TO DISGUISE you," said Dr. Snailwater. "You can't stay shut up in here forever, not if we're to get you home."

Home. Already it seemed distant to Jack, far more so than simply on the other side of a door. Home was a large house and Mrs. Pond. Or it was a cluster of schoolrooms and dormitories and the booming voice of Headmaster Adams. It was deep in the countryside, or it was London.

But this was London, too. Almost. *Londinium.*

"We can't do an arm or a leg," the doctor was saying. "Much too complicated, unless you'd be willing to lose one of your own. No? Well, yes, I can quite understand. Something, however. Hmmm. Aaaah."

Jack wasn't entirely certain he liked the sound of that, but Dr. Snailwater did make a point. There was nothing for the pink of his skin, where everyone else was so pale. He thought of the brass grille worn by the man whom he'd asked for directions to Mayfair, as if getting home were so very simple as that even then.

"Eyes closed." Dr. Snailwater sounded so like Mrs. Pond in tone that Jack did as he was told at once.

Hands washed.

It was cold, so cold against his skin, and a metallic smell strong enough to taste. A leather strap was fastened around the back of his head, pulling at his hair.

"What say you, Beth?" asked the doctor, and Jack took this as permission to open his eyes again. The workshop was dark as a fib, the thick glass of the goggles smudging the truth. Brass rims dug into the soft part of his cheeks and above his eyebrows; his head pitched forward from the weight.

"Very smart," said Beth. "Add a topper and his own mum won't know him. Oh! I do beg your pardon, Jack." Through the glass, he could see one of her hands clapped over her mouth.

"Remember your lessons, Beth, my dear." He frowned. "Perfect brain, perfect size, best materials I could find," he said to Jack, "but still sometimes says things she oughtn't."

"It's all right," Jack mumbled, remembering the time that Mother had come to fetch him from school and had not, in fact, recognized him among the cluster of boys.

A hat was placed on his head, too big but held up quite conveniently by the goggles. It sank down only a little at the back. Beth's key was wound up to its tightest, and out the door the three slipped, off on what Dr. Snailwater would only describe as "a fool's errand, and an errand to visit a fool."

"Ohh, I know," said Beth. The doctor smiled.

It was the first opportunity since he'd met Beth that Jack had to truly look at Londinium, its cobblestones and clockwork and steam, and to appreciate what he was seeing. The goggles made it difficult, but still he could make out the enormous carriages, loud as thunder, reckless as racehorses, though not the writing on their sides. At home those were for perfectly ordinary things, like toothpaste and red currant jam, but he did not think that would be the case here. His head grew damp beneath the hat; the air choked his lungs. Everywhere, positively *everywhere*, there were people, clanking and jangling and peering through bulbous eyes of colored glass or goggles like his own.

None of them gave a second glance to Jack, though several doffed their caps at the doctor, and one or two made quick, jerky bows to Beth. Many wore large masks over their mouths and noses, screened with silks or fine mesh.

Jack wished he could see everything at once. He raised his heavy head and promptly jumped.

"What is that?"

"Hmmm?" Dr. Snailwater turned his head about until he caught what Jack was on about. "Yes, yes, shameful. Have some decency, you filthy layabout." The gargoyle grinned through steely lips, waved a bottle of brown liquor from its perch above a door, and belched out a cloud of steam. "Fascinating creatures, lots to learn, curious dimensions, of course, but they're often guilty of brandy. Mixed with oil, of course, and then they just loll around making the place look untidy."

Jack kept it in his sight as long as he could, so he was nearly walking backward. He'd seen gargoyles before, but they'd been of stone, not smooth metal, and statues shouldn't move like that. . . .

Along the high street they went. Jack strained to see inside shop windows, filled with bundles of herbs he couldn't pronounce, a cage of clockwork imps, each tall and thin, a foot high, hopping on bandy copper legs. A sign promised each to be good at household chores and unfailingly loyal.

He felt dizzy. The strain of the goggles and squinting through them made his head ache, but he couldn't stop looking, not for all the shillings in the country.

"To the Underground!" cried Dr. Snailwater, leading them to a flight of stairs set into the pavement.

This, Jack knew of. They had it in his London, but Mother had never let him travel on it. It was filthy, she said, and full of rats.

He followed Beth and the doctor, grinning. Wherever he was being taken didn't matter. He knew the secret of the clock, and he would never tell, and he would stay here forever, sleeping in the goggles and smearing his pink face with soot if he must.

Down they went, into the station where Dr. Snailwater put coins into a hissing, spitting machine until a pair of gates parted. Down again, to a platform littered here and there with people who paid them no mind.

But Jack watched them from behind the heavy glass. Tried to guess which parts of them were not made of flesh and bone.

"Stay close." A deep rumble shook the floor, a whistle sounded, and the doctor had to shout to be heard. Steam filled the platform so Jack could not even see his hand before his face when he lifted it to try. Bodies brushed past his, and a momentary pang of fear shot through him.

Beth took his arm and led him onto the train. Inside, the air was almost clear, and he could see as Dr. Snailwater led them to a compartment exactly like those Jack rode in to and from school. Rough cloth lined the seats, and lamps burned on the walls. Beth made herself comfortable— though Jack didn't know if she could be *un*comfortable— on a bench and folded her hands in her lap. He sat beside her, the doctor on the other side.

The compartment door slid shut, the whistle blew again, and slowly they began to move.

"How far does it go?"

Beth stared out the window, though beyond there was nothing but darkness. "The train?"

"The Empire."

Dr. Snailwater tilted his shaggy head to one side. "How far does *yours* go?" he asked, in that way that usually means the person doesn't expect an answer.

Across the oceans, to lands for which Jack had only seen maps, heard tales of savages and gentlemen. He wiped a film of soot from his goggles and asked no more questions.

He thought of the miniature train in the parlor and wondered if perhaps he was in a model of a city, laid out on a giant's table. Likely not, but it didn't seem so much of a fantastic idea as it once would have.

It turned out they were going only a few stops. Soon they were fighting their way through the steam again, nearly blind until they reached stairs to take them back up to the street.

Jack's heart sputtered. Above the rooftops loomed the clock tower.

"Don't dawdle, lad."

Beth quickened her steps, and Jack had little choice but to do likewise. He could slow, slip away down an alley and lose them, but the Empire of Clouds seemed a much brighter adventure with Beth and the doctor to help, to feed him and give him a warm bed at night.

Lorcan might not, if Jack could find him, and he was the only other person Jack knew in this place. If he was as mean as they said . . .

He simply had to hope he was right about the clock.

It looked precisely the same. The whole Palace of Westminster did. The same as the one Jack had approached, following Mr. Havelock the magician, who was Sir Lorcan here. The same as the one he had left in a storm, as yet unaware and running to find Mrs. Pond.

It was not raining now, and the people and the faeries and the slurring gargoyles were out, hurrying along the streets and waiting for the motorcars to pass.

"Doctor?"

He looked indulgently at Beth. "Yes, my dear?"

"What time is it?"

And she had called *him* stupid. There was an enormous clock right overhead, but as Jack looked up and opened his mouth, he could see why she had asked.

It was most certainly not eighteen minutes past seven, morning or eve.

"Thing has a mind of its own," said Dr. Snailwater, pulling out a pocket watch. "Always has. Half past one, Beth. Let's go."

They crossed to the iron gates surrounding the palace. It felt much longer than a day since Jack had been here last. Suddenly he wasn't so sure. Merely hoping.

"All right there, lad?"

He nodded slowly.

"Well, in you go, then. Let's try it."

Their eyes on his back, Jack walked through the gates and up to the wall where the door had appeared for Lorcan, and for him. With nothing but the clattering noises of the city now, he put his hand to the stone.

And waited. In his mind, he imagined the cracks growing, splitting to form a door. He'd had the magic to make it appear the first time. Did he have magic to make it stay away if he didn't want it?

Perhaps.

Perhaps not.

Nothing happened.

"I'm not surprised." Dr. Snailwater frowned at the tower and at Jack, as if they'd both displeased him. Possibly they had. But Beth clapped her hands together; there was a noise like ringing bells, not like the great one with the silly name, but of the type cabbies hung on horses at Christmas.

Jack tried to hide his smile.

They did not linger at the tower. The doctor seemed to think it was a good idea to leave in a hurry, dash back to the Underground. But they didn't return to Harleye Street. Instead, they boarded a train, just like the first, headed east out of the city's heart.

This train didn't stay underground. It rose with a jolt,

up, up to run beside the river. Rain began to fall, clearing the fog and spattering the windows in long drops. Jack pressed his goggles to the window, desperate to see everything.

The train slowed to a stop, but Jack paid no attention to the passengers boarding and disembarking. Beyond the window, a tall stone column rose from the ground—the Monument he'd once climbed with Mrs. Pond, except that it wasn't the same one, really. And something about it wasn't right at all.

"It's wrong," he said to Beth and the doctor. "The top's all different. It's not s'posed to be like that. At home it's an urn, not a—"

"Shush!" said the doctor. A wrinkled man eyed them curiously, and Jack felt the blood drain from his face, beneath the goggles that were meant to disguise him. "Addled," said Dr. Snailwater to the man. "Lad doesn't know what he's saying half the time. I'm his doctor, escorting him to the asylum."

Jack opened his mouth, but said nothing.

"Indeed," rasped the man through dry lips, peering at Jack. "Do you know what they'll do to you at the asylum, boy? Oh, there's no fixing you. No, no. Tie you up in straps and leave you to rot. Oh, yes, they will, just like you deserve." He grasped his case and fled through the compartment door, presumably in search of more desirable company.

"I'm not mad," said Jack.

Dr. Snailwater shook his head. "Better mad than discovered, lad."

They passed the rest of the journey in silence, finally alighting in the East End. Here the streets were darker even in what passed for daylight, busier, the buildings even more worn. If the center of the city was a grand lady, bejeweled and gowned in silk, the slums were an old pantomime dame, greasepaint smeared, paste rubies falling from her shoes to run like blood in the gutters.

Here the men reeked of sweat, and ladies' dresses were old and torn. Jack saw a fellow, arm ending at the elbow, no coin to replace it with one of Dr. Snailwater's clever metal hands. Children, bone-thin and dressed in rags, ran barefoot to cadge a mug of water from an old, toothless woman seated behind a rusted bucket. One sat at the curb, nursing a cut leg.

Her veins ran black.

Dr. Snailwater stopped, knelt by the girl, and reached into his fat leather bag for a bandage. It took him only a minute or two; then he gave her a penny and sent her on her way.

"Stay close," he ordered Jack and Beth. Jack had no

intention of doing otherwise as they burrowed deeper into the knot of crooked, rank streets. Tables spilled from a public house onto the cobbles, crowded with broken souls and covered with glasses of beer and lemonade and sour milk. THE FOWLE & FYRE, read a cracked sign above a faded painting of a golden bird in a wreath of flame. Drunken men, half flesh, half rusted metal, stumbled from the door and away into the maze of narrow lanes.

Even in his London, Jack would never have been taken to such a place. There were no feathers here, no gilt chandeliers and conservatories tinkling with the rainfall of piano keys. No housekeepers to bake cake every day, no sons sent off to prepare for careers in Parliament or the Crown or to take over the family business.

They turned into an alley so narrow they had to walk one behind another, the doctor leading with his quick, snappy steps, Beth skipping at Jack's back. Cracked walls loomed, blocking out even the ash-blackened sky. Sunlight would have no hope.

It seemed to Jack nothing here had a hope. He found it strange that a man as fine—if slightly eccentric—as Dr. Snailwater would have even a passing acquaintance with anyone in this horrible, dismal, fascinating place, but the doctor moved quickly and surely.

"He has a pistol in his satchel," Beth whispered.

That, thought Jack, was useful only if he knew how to use it.

A slime-covered archway sat at the end of the alley. Mushrooms shaped like mouths bit at them on their way through, a long, dewy tongue catching Jack's cheek. He wiped it with the back of his hand, and both spots began to tingle.

"Not poisonous," assured Dr. Snailwater. He frowned. "For the most part, at any rate." He led the way through an overgrown courtyard, the air humid enough to drink. In the corner, a faery stomped on a lone flower and laughed a sound like broken glass. The house, if it could be called that, looked assembled from whatever scraps of steel and brick could be filched, and the door had no knocker, no number, no name. It was not a place to be happened upon by chance.

Splinters flew from the wood with each rap from the doctor's metal hand. Jack doubted anyone was home, was sure they must have come all this way for nothing, rather than whatever the *something* was that the doctor wouldn't reveal. Five minutes they stood there, making the most frightful racket, but neither the doctor nor Beth grew disheartened, though Jack conceded that with Beth, at least, it might be difficult to tell.

"Xenocrates! Visitors! Stop being rude and let us in," called the doctor.

A floorboard creaked within. The doorknob turned, and slowly the rotting plank swung open. "You *are* persistent," said a voice. A man stepped from the gloom into the slightly-less-gloom of the doorway. Jack edged behind Beth. Bulging eyes, one brown glass, one blue with a deep crack down the middle, bubbled from scaly, sickly skin. Where there *was* skin. It ended at his cheeks, melting into a brass jaw studded with ivory teeth. The skin reappeared just above his grubby collar.

He caught Jack staring. "The last gent who tried to give me a walloping regretted it. Who's this, then?" he asked Dr. Snailwater, who laughed.

"Stop provoking them, old friend. Jack, meet Xenocrates Fink. Xeno, meet Jack Foster. He is in need of your assistance."

CHAPTER TEN

Possibilities

T HE RAMSHACKLE HOUSE was cleaner inside than Jack had expected, though Mrs. Pond would have fainted at the cobwebs in the corners and half-empty teacups on the tables.

Books lined all of the walls. The sitting room smelled of snow and ink, of will-o'-the-wisps and moonlight. A tailless cat slept on an armchair. Tiny vials of oily, jewel-colored liquids hung from a burning lamp. A faery flew in a broken window to drink from a violet one. A globe spun of its own accord on a wooden stand, but it bore almost no resemblance to ones Jack had seen back home.

This showed only the countries of the Empire, afloat in a sea of blue. As if someone had scraped off the others and left only the island on which he stood and a few more, far away.

"Xeno, here, and I have what you might term *overlapping interests,*" said Dr. Snailwater.

"*You* might say that," answered Xenocrates Fink.

"And I would be correct, as I almost always am."

"Hark who thinks much of himself!"

Beth nudged the cat away and sat down in its place. It stalked off, mewling, as she picked up a book spread open on the chair's arm. Jack removed his goggles, but the spine was too faded to read.

"As I was saying"—the doctor cleared his throat—"overlapping interests. Both scientists, but where I busy myself with the far more sensible nuts and bolts, as it were, his focus is on the more, ah, ethereal arts."

"Xeno made me alive," said Beth, not looking up from her book.

"And a splendid job he did, for without him you'd be an unthinking automaton, good only for the shipyards."

"How, Mr. Fink? How do you do it?" asked Jack. He had not known, until now, that the doctor needed any help, that it wasn't simply a matter of finding the right gears in his workshop.

"Xeno, if you please. No airs here. A little of this, a little of that. Keep the faeries happy with their nectars—flavored oils, lavender, nutmeg—and they'll help. Give a pinch of magic just where it's needed. Now, what need you from me? Not a soul, unless my eyes do me wrong." He laughed bitterly through his teeth. "A brain? Are you by chance a nitwit?"

"No," said Jack, scowling.

"We need to know about doorways, Xeno. Young Jack here's found himself on the wrong side of one."

"Risky business," said Xeno.

"I didn't do it on purpose." Except that, in a manner of speaking, Jack had. Jack fell silent as Dr. Snailwater laid out the tale, or as much as he knew of it. Every now and then, Xeno would leap to pull a book from a shelf, the crack in the blue eye sliding over the words.

"No luck when you tried to go back?"

Jack watched another faery, small as a dragonfly, sip from emerald oil. "No," he said carefully.

"Hmmm. I shall make inquiries. Quietly, of course. Best keep him hidden or disguised, Snailwater. Lorcan's a right nasty piece of work, just like his mistress. The pair of them, wanting to take us to war with the colonies, as if we don't have problems here."

"That's enough," said the doctor, glancing at Jack and Beth.

"Yes, yes, of course. Now, you simply must tell me about your land." Xeno cleared a stack of papers from a chair and ushered Jack into it, brass jaw grinning. A light glowed behind his eyes.

"Uh, all right." And so he did, what he knew, what he'd learned from school and Mrs. Pond and eavesdropping on elegant suppers after he was sent to bed. Xeno sat fascinated, and even Beth put down her book as Jack described electric lights.

To them, it seemed that was magic. But Jack thought it boring compared to the faeries and clockwork, the people here with their bits of metal all over.

A thing occurred to him, swimming from the back of his mind to the front.

"D'you think there are others? Doorways, I mean."

Xeno had no lips to put together in thought, but it seemed as though he would have, if it were possible. Dr. Snailwater ran his real hand through the fluff atop his head, and Beth waited.

Suddenly, Xeno laughed. Wheezy and harsh, his ivory teeth clacking together.

"Others? Of course there must be. Somewhere out there could be a world run by water, or sunlight. Buildings could hang from the sky, the people doing their shopping upside down. The key"—he spread his arms, and a steel faery lit on his rumpled shirtsleeve—"is to accept that anything is possible."

• • •

Xeno fed them a lunch of bread and cheese, a jug of cold water beside to wash the slick grime from Jack's mouth and throat. Beth ate nothing, but a cup of oil was set out for her and she drank dutifully. The doctor bickered with Xeno until only crumbs remained on the table, their words fast and so laden with interruptions Jack gave up trying to follow the conversation.

"You know," said Xeno, setting down his knife. "There is one possibility—"

"No, there is not," answered the doctor, a knowing look in his eye. "You cannot still be playing conkers with *that* old chestnut. It is a *myth*, old friend, and you will not give the lad false hope."

"What's a myth?"

"It's a kind of story," Beth offered.

"I know *that*," said Jack. Clearly she still thought he was a bit stupid. "I mean, what are you talking about, Xeno?"

"Never you mind." The doctor fixed Jack with a firm stare. "Beth, why don't you take him outside."

Beth led him through a tiny, cluttered kitchen to a bit of garden, better kept than the courtyard. Powder-winged butterflies flew in clusters with metal ones. Enormous flowers bloomed in a blinding riot of color. More of the tongued mushrooms clung to the walls, snapping at one another.

Overhead, the sky was almost night black, the thick clouds trapping the city lights, providing enough to see by.

He wanted to ask Beth what the myth was. Surely she knew, but that would make it sound as if he wanted to go home. As if he wanted hope, false or not. So he kept silent, watching as she puttered around the flower beds.

A faery, no bigger than his thumb, caught his eye as it scampered up to poke at his shoe. Through the stiff leather, he couldn't feel it, no matter how hard the creature tried.

Jack leaned down, putting his hand close by, as Wilson had taught him to catch lady birds. The faery tilted its face up to Jack, and it looked very nearly human, eyes and nose and mouth all of steel but otherwise just like a person's. It climbed slowly onto his palm, and Jack carefully, very slowly, straightened up, raising it to eye level.

"Hello," he said. The faery watched him with curiosity, but none of the pinching, poking nastiness he'd seen from others. Perhaps Xeno's oily nectars tamed the ones who lived back here.

It didn't answer him, but turned in a circle, tiny feet tickling Jack. Filigreed wings fluttered, not quick enough to set it to flight.

Unlike Beth, the faery had none of what might be called *skin*, but it was easy to see how she might look something like this beneath it. Every bone carefully formed, hinges at knee, elbow, and knuckle. The thinnest filaments sprouting out of its head as hair.

Would it hurt if he took it apart? He'd put it back together, of course, but possibly it was cruel to do such a thing. Who fixed them if they broke, or could they fix themselves, or one another?

Magic as they were, Jack wondered if it wouldn't be simpler to be made this way.

"Oy!" He scowled at Beth as she ran to him, footsteps heavy, and the faery squeaked, springing up to the air, flying out of sight.

Beth shrugged, unbothered. "There's loads. You'll catch another."

But there was no chance to catch another so that he could puzzle out how they worked. Dr. Snailwater poked his head out the door to call them inside so they could take their leave. Xeno bowed them from the house, and Jack remembered what he had said not long before: that anything was possible.

Jack pondered this all the way back to Harleye Street. They took the train once more, slightly less disorienting this time now he knew what to expect.

Up again on the street, the day's soot hung thick and black. There'd been no rain to wash it away. Through the goggles, Jack looked at the homes and offices and Londinium's towers that poked up through the clouds like pins, their tops hidden completely.

He was a bit tired, and his chest hurt with each breath.

But anything was possible. He could learn magic, or clockwork, and here those things were not so different as in London, but rather entwined, feeding off each other. Mechanical creatures that flew and thought for themselves, mystery and wonder grounded in the metal that was everywhere.

It was silly to think he had to stay hidden. That was hardly any different than what his mother did, and besides, not a single person had said anything about how pink he was, not the whole time he'd been out.

He wanted to be having adventures, exploring. There was so much to see, through the thick glass of his borrowed goggles or not. He wanted to know how everything was put together. How all of it *worked*.

Dr. Snailwater's was filled with clanking, chugging noises as they stepped into the workshop. Upstairs, the train ran around the room, taking its passengers on their journey to nowhere and back again.

"I've a few things to do downstairs," said the doctor when they'd shucked coats and shoes—and—in Jack's case—goggles and topper. "No mischief up here, now."

But Jack didn't want to sit around. "Can I help?" he asked.

Dr. Snailwater gave him an appraising sort of look. "All right. Let's see if you're any good with this sort of thing, as you say. Any mucking about and it's straight back up here with you, mind."

Jack nodded seriously. Beth followed them, finding a stool in the corner from which to watch. The doctor laid out boxes of screws and tiny brass whatnots, plates and cogs and wheels. A cloth bag held all manner of tools, from hammers big as Jack's arm to wrenches small as sewing needles.

"What are we doing?"

"Aha." From inside a burlap sack trapped beneath one of the tables, Dr. Snailwater produced a foot. He set it on the worktop, and before their eyes, it hopped its way over to the edge, then fell to the floor with a *clang*.

"Catch it, would you, lad? It won't stop doing that. The owner isn't best pleased with tap-dancing everywhere all the day and night. Told him I'd take a gander."

Jack returned with the foot, which wasn't exactly easy to carry since it kept trying to jump away. He held it fast as the doctor quickly removed part after part, setting them out in rows until the thing gave a last, forlorn little kick and was finally motionless, half of it still a maze of metal.

"Right then. It's possible something tainted it, a bit of

faery business or whatnot, and now it's taken on a life of its own, but we'll try the usual things first. Here, lad"—the doctor pressed a turnscrew into Jack's hand—"show me how you'd sort it out."

They were waiting for him to do something silly. Not because they were unkind; on the contrary, Dr. Snailwater had been very kind, and Beth was all right for a girl without a heart, but he was a stranger here.

Jack took stock of all the pieces: screws and bars, the slightly curved bits that were clearly toenails, the chunk the doctor hadn't disassembled. The other machines in the room chugged away in time with his thoughts.

The cogs slotted neatly into each other; the wheels spun with a simple flick. All the noise, the clutter, the feeling of eyes on him faded away.

He chose a turnscrew from Dr. Snailwater's tools and set to work on the rest of the foot.

Odd, really, to think that it was a foot. A man walked on this, went about his day, perhaps removed it nightly for sleep and surely put it out of harm's way while bathing.

One by one, the pieces came away, until only a small knot of metal parts, screwed so tight they were nearly a solid lump, remained on the table.

"Need a hand, lad?" the doctor asked.

Jack wiped his forehead on his shirtsleeve. "No," he

answered, gasping with the effort of loosening the screws. A cog came away, clunking to the table.

Something hissed. A pink mist billowed. Sparks flared and died within it.

"Beth. A jar, if you please. Hurry."

Jack stared at the cloud rising above the worktop as Beth handed a small, heavy-lidded jar to the doctor. A quick swipe, and the odd pink stuff was trapped, humming, fizzing against the glass.

"That rather explains it," said the doctor.

"What is it?" Jack watched more sparks burst. "Faery magic?"

"Don't know as you'd call it magic, really. Not if everything's got a soul. Bit got trapped where it shouldn't be, that's all. Not enough to be a whole one. Doubt the creature's missing it."

"How . . . How big is a whole one?"

"Depends. Needs about a brandy bottle for a faery, bigger for a person. Glad we got that sorted. You've not done a bad job, lad. Think you can put it all back together?"

Jack thought so, and did. It was fiddly work, and once or twice the doctor cleared his throat, so as to let Jack know he was about to use the wrong piece, but in a very kind way. Finally, the foot, complete and still and gleaming from a quick polish, was back in its burlap sack under the table.

Dr. Snailwater served a thick stew for supper for himself and Jack, another cup of oil for Beth. Soon after, her hands began to slow and words to slur. She settled herself in an armchair and went still, hands folded over her pretty, frayed dress. Dr. Snailwater dragged an enormous copper tub into the kitchen and filled it with pan after pan of hot water for Jack.

Even the soap was black, but it lathered well enough, and it felt lovely to be clean.

The nightdress fell to his ankles, striped like a prisoner's uniform.

He selected a book—F. Z. Montague's *The Personages of Starlight*—for no reason other than it was close by. It was cozy, with the fire lit, the scent of stew still filling the room. Back in London, he would've been sent to bed by now, hidden away while his parents entertained, not sat in a lovely warm room, reading in companionable silence with a strange doctor and an even stranger windup girl. He read until Beth wound down and the doctor bade him good night, then fell into his blankets and slept a peaceful sleep.

CHAPTER ELEVEN

A Plan in Motion

WHEN THE FIRST MAN WAS hanged, Lorcan merely watched. It was no one of any importance, a subject simply plucked off the street. The rope around his neck, he fell with such force that the grille dislodged from his nostrils and bounced away, clattering against the wooden boards.

Only a few people were there to watch, but word would spread. Fear would ripple across the city, and that fear would be loud enough to reach the boy, wherever he hid.

Indeed, it would be simpler now than convincing the fool to let him go ever was, or spiriting the child away from his London home in the dead of night. A plan was beginning to form in his head, based on his own secret knowledge.

And when Lorcan planned and plotted, it was with all the methodical accuracy of a man who has had many lifetimes to perfect his craft. He had led armies to war and emerged victorious, built this London to match the other for the Lady's happiness, kept his own secrets hidden where none would ever find them.

There was no point now in attempting to find out just how the boy had come to gain entry through Lorcan's doorway. The hair taken from his bedchamber had been enough to give Lorcan the briefest of glimpses, enough to show that the boy had slipped through the door.

Small hands upon the stone where Lorcan's had been seconds before. The cracks growing.

He would only have had to turn around, just once, and the boy would have been his.

Lorcan swore. The footman at the throne room door jumped in surprise.

However perplexing, the boy was *here*, and that made it all so much easier, even as the idea was worrying.

Lorcan could not help but think that he had chosen perhaps too well; the boy had some kind of magic in him; that was the only explanation. Still, that would please the Lady when the boy was hers, as he would be soon.

And it was helpful. Now there was just the matter of providing a bit of incentive.

"Lorcan," said the Lady as he entered. "News?"

"None yet, Lady." But soon, soon. Surely the boy would come.

"Bring him to me, Lorcan. I am tired of waiting."

"Yes, Lady." But if Lorcan's plan worked, he would not have to find the boy. The boy would come to him.

Out on the street, he raised his hand and pointed to a passerby, pretty in a plum-colored dress. "That one." He did not watch the palace guards grab her, or her struggles as she realized what they were doing. He heard her kicks, her screams, through the window of his carriage until the driver started the engine. The hiss of steam obscured all.

It was a short journey to the gallows, where a larger crowd than the day before had gathered. Good. Very good. Of course, they were there to witness the hanging out of relief that it was not their own necks that would snap, but Lorcan could hardly blame them for that.

He felt only anticipation.

Minutes later, the rope swung, the woman, too. Lorcan lingered only long enough to confirm her passing.

He hoped he'd need no longer than that. Any child with a heart would want to make it stop, surely. A heart to love the Lady. That had been the problem with the failed experiments of that fool doctor.

Stepping away from the gallows, grime-slick cobbles underfoot, he made his way to his carriage, cloaked in gossamer steam.

Such a beautiful city. Pride filled him. The people busy, everywhere the hum and thrum of industry. Everywhere else, the delicate magic that had come before him. The same magic that ensured he would live as long as the faeries.

As long as the Lady. Forever, he would give her everything she wished, even if he didn't want to, as a good son ought.

So first, the boy.

The carriage deposited him a few minutes from his destination, for it was never wise to let the lowly foot soldier behind the wheel see him approach the tower.

As he walked, he withdrew from his pocket a small device obtained from a metallurgist and swaddled in layers of protective cloth.

For one second, measured by the clock overhead, he considered visiting London, the other city, one final time. No. There was no need.

His fingers began to tingle with warmth as he neared. Blackened trees along the river shivered, starred with the silver specks of resting birds. The cloth flew away as he turned the clockwork contraption over in his hand, careful not to shake it hard enough to break the vial of kerosene inside.

Lorcan wound the key that would release the spark. Just enough to give him time to step away from the wall where the doorway would no longer be after five . . . four . . .

It was not a terribly large explosion. Stone flew and smashed on the ground.

Oh, well. He would send someone to repair it later, completely new, its powers lost. The tower itself was still safe and strong, far too well made to be felled by the small destruction.

It took several minutes to climb the stairs, up into the sky burning with sunset, red and gold. Heat crawled along his skin. He had removed the clock parts from his pockets, returned them to their rightful places, and it ticked loud now in his ears.

The boy had magic in him, an affinity at least, or he would never have found the doorway. And Lorcan had his own, never stronger than in this spot, looking out over the grand city he had made for the Lady. He didn't need to come here to make this particular magic work, but it felt right to do so, somehow. The boy had sneaked into the Empire directly below where Lorcan stood. He took a deep breath. He had never done this before, the risk that someone might discover how he was able to was too great, but it was worth that risk to get the boy, who surely had not learned the legend. Lorcan had no doubt the boy would hear.

"Come to me."

The clock began to chime.

CHAPTER TWELVE
And the Gallows Swung

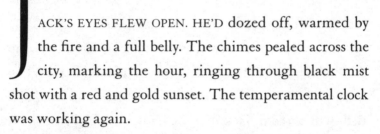

J ACK'S EYES FLEW OPEN. HE'D dozed off, warmed by the fire and a full belly. The chimes pealed across the city, marking the hour, ringing through black mist shot with a red and gold sunset. The temperamental clock was working again.

Come to me. I know you are here, little Jack Foster.

He blinked. "Who said that?" he asked.

Dr. Snailwater looked at him, puzzled, from an armchair. "What, lad?"

"I thought I heard . . ." No, he knew he'd heard the voice, a man's voice, and it seemed he'd heard it in his dream, too. But perhaps it wouldn't be clever to say so out loud. It would be the asylum for him, just as the man on the train by the Monument had said. All tied up in a strait-jacket until his bones thinned and crumbled and his lungs turned black.

I know you are here, the voice in his head repeated. *I have destroyed the doorway and you will never return home. Come to me, below the clock. You will be the most precious son of the Empire of Clouds.*

The voice stopped, and Jack let out his breath. Destroyed the doorway? Well, that was all fine and good, if it was true. He didn't want to go back anyway.

The first two were not your fault. You weren't to know, but now you do. One each day, little Jack. Their blood will be on your hands. One each day until you come to me.

Jack's whole body began to tremble. He didn't need to think about what the voice meant. The hangings. When word of the first had come, the doctor shook his head and Beth whispered to Jack that the Lady must be upset about something or other. Five, ten, twenty people would meet their ends before the Lady grew tired and moved on to something else.

"Are you all right, lad? You look pale as one of us."

"Yes," Jack whispered.

But he most assuredly was not.

• • •

The third hanging drew ten thousand spectators, all in bright finery, rings glinting on pointed fingers—or the hands themselves catching the light.

For the fourth, tickets were sold, and people jostled one another for the best view. Rumor had it that the profits would pay to add another airship to the fleet Jack had seen flying on his first afternoon in the Empire.

The city grew dark with fear. Xeno visited briefly and was roundly shouted at by the doctor for walking the streets alone. The pockets of street urchins grew heavy with coins, payment for escorting anyone who could afford it safely to their destination.

Jack read all of this in the papers until Dr. Snailwater took them away, saying young eyes didn't need to see such things.

But Jack *did* need to see. The hangings were his fault. The voice had said so.

He still hadn't told the doctor or Beth about the voice. Jack knew what happened to mad people, and it sounded no better here than in London. Possibly worse. All their metal and clockwork couldn't fix sicknesses of the mind.

Come to me.

It was Lorcan's voice, Jack knew. Remembered it from listening at the keyhole to Mother's parlor. Every night, right at sunset, the faeries gathered beneath the gas lamps and the people gathered at the gallows and Lorcan spoke to Jack as the clock chimed.

You can put an end to this.

And then the gallows swung. Jack huddled in fusty blankets of mothskin and dust and tried not to picture the moment the rope dropped. The trapdoor would fall and the wood would creak, the man or woman would gasp and gasp. Perhaps their hands were bound at their backs to keep from pulling at the noose. Their feet, however, those would be free, and they'd kick out, scrabbling for purchase on the slick, oily air.

Come to me, little Jack, and it will stop.

He covered his ears, earning himself an odd look from the doctor, a mildly curious one from Beth, but it didn't help even a bit, anyway.

"How sad it must be for their families," said Beth, kicking her heels as Jack and Dr. Snailwater bent over an arm in the workshop. "I'm going upstairs to read."

"Bless her," said the doctor fondly, measuring the elbow. "She does try. Sometimes I wonder if I taught her too well; to this day she worries about the Lady because it's the kind thing to do, even if the Lady doesn't deserve the concern. Beth is most definitely my best work."

"She said there were others. Twelve of them."

"Hmm. Needs another three quarters of an inch. Yes, others, yes."

"Where?"

The doctor dug about in his tools for a moment. "All in bits now," he said rather sadly. "I don't like to tell her that. Girl may not have a heart, but she has a soul, finest Xeno could get. It would frighten Beth to think someone might do the same to her."

"They won't?"

"I won't permit it. She's not hurting anyone, is she, now? Brightens the place up, having her hang about with that smile always on her face."

It dawned on Jack that without himself and Beth here, the doctor would spend a great deal of time alone. He didn't even have a woman to keep for him, like Mrs. Pond, much less a wife and family of his own. Beth must be something of a daughter to him, in her way.

Jack opened his mouth and closed it again. No, he mustn't say a word about the voice, or admit that he had known how to get home but couldn't now because Lorcan had destroyed the doorway. Either the doctor would think him mad, or dangerous, or he'd believe Jack, which was danger of another kind. He might cast Jack out into the street, fearing that Lorcan would somehow come to find him in the workshop.

Most of all, Jack didn't want to admit that he could stop the hangings, if he wished, but hadn't yet. It made him ill to think about.

So he passed Dr. Snailwater a turnscrew when asked and did the more finicky bits—for which Jack's small hands were an advantage—and said nothing.

"Tell me about her. The Lady, I mean."

Beth looked up from her book. A lunch of bread and cheese shot through with green churned through Jack's belly. In his head, the rope was swinging, swinging.

"She's not so very terrible, not at first. Very pretty, she is." Beth stood to help a tiny gentleman who had dropped his case getting onto the model train. "She tries, you know. I would brush her hair and she'd send for cake, but I couldn't eat it, 'course. And then she'd turn ugly. Not really, but her face'd be terribly angry and twisted, and she'd run to her rooms. You could hear the door slamming all through the palace. I was there for nearly a whole year, and at the end every day was like that, because she tries so very hard for things to be perfect and fun, and when they're not, she doesn't know what to do."

"She sounds like a child," said Jack, thinking of the hiding Mrs. Pond would give him if he acted in such a way.

Beth's eyelids clicked, a blink. "Oh, no," she said. "I

think she's just so very old she's never had to act like a grown-up. At any rate, there's the most loveliest library. I'd go and read until she came to find me again. The doctor thinks it upset her that I was never bothered overmuch by her tantrums."

The afternoon newspapers came, hitting the door with an enormous thump. Jack looked out the window to see an imp on a bicycle, trailing steam as it sped along the street, the creature aiming the papers at each house.

HANGING NUMBER SIX: RECORD AUDIENCE PREDICTED, it read.

Jack tried to console himself with the thought that the Lady had done this before, or so Beth said. It wasn't really his fault, not if she had people hanged whenever she was angry.

"Doesn't look like rain. Fancy a walk? Oh, don't look like such a Nellie. You'll be fine with your goggles and topper."

In a careful hand, Beth left a note for the doctor to find when he returned from the market with food for himself and Jack. The goggles blurred the words and turned the world to smudges, letting through only the most vivid colors. The ladies on the street in their sweet-shop dresses, all lemon drops and strawberry trifles and peppermints, the hems streaked with muck. The air could hardly be deemed *fresh*, but it was a relief to be out, exploring, forgetting for a brief time words printed in inky headlines and rattling around his head.

He suspected the doctor wouldn't be very happy that they'd ventured out without him, and this was a thrill all by itself. Jack had never had anyone to get in trouble with before. Mrs. Pond was very fond of saying he did a good job of that all by himself.

Freshly wound and oiled, Beth walked quickly, neat buckled shoes clicking on the pavement. Jack hurried to keep up. Faeries skated over the grime on the street, wings shining. A barrow boy sold apples red as poison, a smile on his face as he sniffed through the grille at his nose.

Somewhere, music played. A jaunty tune, notes skipping along the fiddle strings.

"Where are we going?" He'd thought, at first, that she must be taking him to the park in which he'd first seen her standing in the birdcage, but realized that was in another direction.

"A surprise!" Her laughter sounded like an armful of copper pipes dropped to the floor.

She led him through streets and alleys, skirting the monstrous carriages that seemed to be everywhere, keeping Jack moving too fast for anyone to get a proper look at him. For nearly an hour they walked, until Jack's chest hurt with breathing. He was about to ask her to stop, just so's he could catch his air, when she did, all of a sudden.

"This way," she commanded, darting into a lane no wider than a grown man's shoulders. Halfway down was a door, rotted through in parts, lock hanging useless and rusted.

They climbed a set of stairs that groaned and sulked with each footfall, winding up past other doors that apparently held no interest to Beth as Jack gasped and wheezed behind her.

The top of the building was one great room with windows at either end, half of them smashed to pieces or filched for the glass. Shards squeaked beneath their shoes. A flock of metal birds crowed, wings ringing as they flew overhead in a circle around a still one in the middle of the floor, separated from its bent wings. Jack didn't know whether to think of it as broken or dead.

He pulled the goggles from his face and wiped the window with his hand. On the street below, a crowd was beginning to form with all the sparkling celebration of a party.

She had brought him to the gallows.

"It's starting. Come see."

Jack's stomach slithered. Beth had fashioned herself a seat from an old crate, brushing the dust from it first so as to not spot her dress. She sat by the window, beckoning to him, and her smile felt out of place amid the glass dust and the squawking.

On the street, the crowd had doubled—nay, tripled. Elbows nudged and jerked. A woman lost her hat. It fell to the ground, was trampled to straw not fit for horses and a sad bit of ribbon.

All heads were turned to the wooden platform. A guard in plumes and brass stood near the noose, occasionally shouting to the people to be silent. They did not listen, if even they heard him at all, until all at once, a hush fell over everyone. A great carriage, snorting steam that swirled around and through the bars on the one high window in back, approached. It stopped in a spot set aside for it behind the gallows. A driver—another guard, plumage just the same—got out.

Jack's breath caught in his sore chest. From nowhere, the first face he recognized appeared.

Here Lorcan did not wear the neat suit in which he'd visited Jack's home under the guise of being Mother's new spiritualist. And of course he knew now that it had been a ruse all along, that what the soft-spoken, intriguing Mr. Havelock had wanted all along was not to summon the dead, but to take away a very-much-alive Jack.

No, here Lorcan wore a rich frock coat of bottle-green

velvet, a flower sprouting from the lapel. His breeches were neatly buckled, boots polished to a shine. On his head, a topper bound in brass cocked slightly to one side.

"Always looks just the same," said Beth. Jack did not answer.

Several more guards nudged the crowd back, so's they could open the doors of the carriage. Jack closed his eyes for a moment, but they would not stay shut no matter how tight he squeezed them.

It was just a man. A man like any other. The sleeve of his thin shirt flapped in the breeze, empty of an arm to keep it in place. Perhaps they had taken the arm, or the man never had enough coin to buy one at all. A uniformed hangman stood beside him.

The guards surrounded him, chivvied him up the stairs. The man's feet did not seem to want to move.

He could stop it. Run down the stairs and out into the crowd, hollering at the top of his lungs for Lorcan, who would know him straightaway. There'd be no need for the noose to be tightened around the man's neck as they were doing just now.

Beth's mouth opened with a click.

Jack turned away, eyes fixed on the bird on the floor. It was already dead. Still, he knew the moment the trapdoor fell away. Twenty thousand gasps and twenty thousand cheers smothering the sound of creaking wood.

"That was much faster than I imagined," said Beth plainly. Crescent-moon bruises purpled on Jack's palms.

"It was horrible," he said. Just the thought was dreadful enough.

She thought about this for a moment. "Yes, yes I suppose it was. I don't understand, you know, not very much. Not being born the way others were, like you were. No chance of me dying same as others, neither."

But Jack listened with only half an ear. The guards were pulling the man from the hole, slipping the rope from a neck that was surely never meant to bend at such an angle. They laid him out on the planks.

His feet still twitched.

A fog like the one that swathed the sky cleared from Jack's mind.

"We should get back. Dr. Snailwater will be missing us," he said, careful to keep his voice very normal, however unlikely it was that Beth would sense a difference at all. They waited until Lorcan had climbed into a carriage, until its stream of smoke was lost around the next corner. A silly precaution, considering, but one that must be made.

Under cover of the departing crowd, Jack once more disguised, they left the gallows and set their aim for

Harleye Street. The sun had dropped below the ash, lending a lightness to the evening it did not quite deserve.

Jack's belly still did not feel right. Whether that was due to what he had seen or what was to come, he wasn't certain. Both, likely.

"I should tar the pair of you," said the doctor the moment they pushed through the door, dropping a hammer with such force the table on which it landed shook. "Gallivanting off like that." His shock of hair was wilder than usual, as if he'd been clutching at it. Jack tugged off the goggles and saw a few white strands trapped in the hinges of Dr. Snailwater's fingers.

"I wanted to go for a walk," said Beth. "We were perfectly safe. Not even a drop of rain."

"Yes, well." The doctor huffed, and Jack knew this was not what he had been concerned about; that his worries were almost certainly closer to the truth than what Beth let on with her sweet, innocent smile. "Upstairs, both. And hands washed, Jack. There's a stew."

It was good stew, rich and thick, brown gravy heavy with carrots and onions, just like the food at school. As was her habit, Beth drank her oil and retired to a chair in the sitting room with a book, reading until her eyes moved too slowly, her fingers sluggish at turning a page. Her key traveled its final few spins, her eyelids dropped.

"I've had word from Xeno," said the doctor, pouring a cup of tea. "He'll be 'round tomorrow."

It would be of no use, whatever Xeno had learned. The doorway was gone, destroyed forever. Jack believed the voice, for it had not lied about the hangings.

He thought of the twitching foot.

"All right," Jack said quietly.

Dr. Snailwater squinted, tapping his brass fingertips against the china. "Hmmm. See yourself to bed now."

The blankets still choked, and Jack lay in his nightclothes, imagining himself climbing the stairs to the noose. All the faces agog, ready to gasp in surprise though they weren't surprised at all. The planks groaned; the rope was rough around his throat. It took the hangman a long while to tighten it, being as Jack's neck was so small, for he was only a boy.

He started awake, ears pricked. No sound, save the usual chugs and clunks, came from the workshop. All the lamps were dark, wicks cooling in the night. Dr. Snailwater had gone to his bed.

In silence, Jack found his shirt, trousers, socks. Beth would not wake, not when he dropped a shoe or from the scratching of the pencil as, on the back of the note she had written earlier in the day, he scribbled his own.

He took nothing with him but for that which he'd worn or had when he'd arrived. The topper and goggles he set on the table beside the crystal ball that wasn't as useless as Dr. Snailwater made it out to be. In his pocket rested the compass Mrs. Pond had bought for him.

Jack could no longer remember how many days ago that was. Perhaps, if he ever found himself home again, it would be to a London where a year, or ten, had passed for every day he'd been gone. And so perhaps it was best that he never would.

Little boys take what they're given and don't complain, said a voice in his head, but it was a friendly one, this time. Mrs. Pond's voice.

Outdoors was heavy with a squirming, darting, fluttering darkness. Creatures moved just beyond reach or sight, except for the tiny faeries who continued their lamp-glow dances.

He did not get lost, or frightened, as often as he'd feared he might. A few times something oily and slurred shouted at him from the shadows, but he quickened his steps and they did not follow.

The clock cloaked itself in ash and cloud. Jack followed the bells rolling over the night, then the river's lazy, rhythmic whisper.

At the base of the tower, two guards stood, feathers in their hats tickling the shreds of light from a nearby streetlamp. Even in the soupy dim Jack could see, behind them, the bright, new wooden door where the magical one had been. Just an ordinary door now.

"And who might you be, then?" asked one of them, peering at Jack. "Bit late for little wretches to be out, isn't it?"

Jack's throat went very dry. "I'm Jack," he said. "You're waiting for me."

Everything seemed to happen at once. A hand clamped down on his shoulder, too pointy to be real. The guard's metal lungs clanked in his chest, breath close to Jack's ear. An imp darted from the shadows to run away in a knife flash of silver.

Moments later, a hammering, rattling dawned and grew louder—a carriage. Jack held his breath. It had scarcely pulled to a stop when the rear door opened.

"Little Jack Foster," said Lorcan. "I knew you would come."

CHAPTER THIRTEEN

The Lady's New Son

P ERFECT, he is."

"Nearly. Bit grubby."

"Bath'll soon sort that out."

The room was filled with chattering Jack only half heard. He was too busy gazing—or perhaps gaping was a better word. Once he'd thought his own house was grand enough, but this was something else entirely. Rich gold covered the walls and ceilings. Steam drifted gently from lamps on silk-covered tables, the light turning the wine color to blood red in spots.

"Wherever did you find him?"

"I shouldn't think," said Lorcan, "that it would be any business of yours."

"Come with me," said a girl. Jack thought of her as a girl in the way that he had been taught to view anyone in an apron as a girl. Except Mrs. Pond.

Lorcan's hand pinched Jack's shoulder hard enough to bruise and let him go.

Jack's heart thudded, but he let the girl nudge him through a set of tall wooden doors. Here a marble floor grew seamlessly into a wide, curved staircase.

"Up you go."

And up he went, to a corridor of closed doors and shadows, of dark portraits and carpet that thirstily drank in both their footsteps.

"This one's yours, fit for a son of the Lady's," said the girl, her hand on a doorknob. Jack felt as if he'd swallowed several of those steel-winged faeries, but he followed her in.

The room shimmered. It was as if he were underwater, in a diving helmet, breathing as blues and greens rippled everywhere around him. Beside an enormous four-poster bed, a tiny dragon sat in a cage, snoring gentle puffs of steam.

The girl caught him looking. "Aye, the Lady wishes you to have a pet," she said. He moved closer. It was about twelve inches high and had hinged wings like the faeries, though bigger and a bit pointier at the ends. Most of the rest of it was a mass of gears and rivets and fiddly things, all covered in small, flat scales. Its head and feet were smooth, rather as if they'd been cast in a mold, though they couldn't have been. As he watched, the creature blinked its red eyes and opened its mouth to yawn.

Jack had never been permitted so much as a kitten back home, and this wondrous thing was ever so much better than a kitten. He stared in awe at its stomping iron feet, the wings that began to flap faster and faster. A hotter, meaner jet of steam issued violently from its nostrils, a high-pitched screech piercing the room. The entire cage rattled against the table.

"I don't think it likes me," said Jack, loud enough for the girl to hear him over the racket. A particularly violent kick from one of the creature's strong legs snapped one of the metal bars that imprisoned it, and the dragon screamed again.

"It likes you fine," said the girl, pushing past Jack, a tiny cup in her hand. She deftly avoided another cloud of scalding steam and poured a ribbon of thick black liquid down into a waiting, thirsty mouth.

So it needed to drink oil, just like Beth did. Had Beth had a dragon during her time here? Perhaps she'd had *this* one. Jack made up his mind to ask her, if he ever saw her again.

They hanged people to get me here.

"I'll run your bath," said the girl. He nodded and did not speak as she opened another door.

The bath was not like the copper tub at Dr. Snailwater's, with water slopping over onto the kitchen floor. Instead, it was an enormous marble thing, brass spouts at one end, the other far enough away Jack thought he might have to swim to it. The whole room was marble, echoing, the splashing of the water so loud he could as well be in the eye of a thunderstorm. Gathered around a sink were bottles and bottles that glowed unearthly colors, sometimes two at once, as if dreams had been captured in the glass and stoppered there.

"I am perfectly capable of bathing myself," said Jack when it looked as if the girl would stay.

Her eyes slanted. "Be right outside, then."

That was well enough. He wasn't a *child*.

The water was warm, but not overly so. His clothes lay in a crumpled heap on the floor, and he had a sneaking suspicion he would never see them again. That they were the last part of him to go.

He stayed in until the bath grew cool, then cold, and he shivered. A clock on the wall—even *his* house did not have such things in the bath—read close to dawn. Beth and Dr. Snailwater would be waking soon. Well, *he* would, and the doctor would wind Beth before making tea, and they would see right away that Jack was gone.

A rich suit of blue, stitched with silver, waited for him,

finer than anything he'd ever worn before. The girl helped him, for there were too many buttons and buckles to count on the shirt and coat and small leather boots. There was a mirror, tall as a man, but Jack did not look.

"What's your name?" Jack asked the girl.

"Arabella, your lordship," she said. "The Lady will be positively chuffed with you. Might give us all a half day."

Jack went over to the cage, put his hand on the lock. Would it fly away? The dragon spread its wings, clanging against the bars.

"Aye, those ones are sweet enough once they've had their oils," said Arabella, "but steer clear of the ones in the mountains. Big as houses, they are. Not that you'll have much need to leave the palace, of course. No risk of steaming for you."

"And the Lady? Is she sweet?" Jack asked.

Arabella's eyes darkened, as if smoke were swirling through the glass. Like marbles. "She will be to you. Such a rage she was in when she thought she'd never get you. Sir Lorc—" She snapped her mouth shut.

"Sir Lorcan what?"

"Never you mind. Your lordship, sir. The Lady is lovely; you'll see."

Lordship. Jack slid the latch free. The door swung open and the dragon whipped its head toward the sound. It leaped for freedom so quickly, Jack jumped back, landing sprawled on the bed. Wings flapped, lifting, soaring up to the ceiling, flashing in the lamplight.

Arabella ducked as it swooped an inch above her head. Twice it circled the room, hissing thin jets of steam from its nostrils. Jack sat up for a better look, and it slowed, drifting down to land on his shoulder.

"Hello," he said. It was lighter than he'd expected, and the thick cloth of his suit protected him from its steely talons.

"See? Best of friends," said Arabella approvingly. "Now, back it goes."

"What would happen if I took it apart?" he asked.

Her eyes widened in glassy shock. "That would be as murder, your lordship," she said.

"Why? Couldn't I just put it together again?"

Arabella shook her head violently. "The pieces'd all be there, but *it* would be gone. Needs to be held together to keep the . . . the essence of it inside, see?"

"Oh." With some difficulty, he prized the creature off and tucked it back inside the cage, locking the door tight.

Far away, deep in the palace, something crashed. Arabella flinched. "Goodness! She's awake. Come. Hurry now."

Hurrying was difficult in the strange new boots with

their little raised heels and toes that pinched a bit. And Jack did not want to go. In this room, this room that was *his* now, everything that had happened thus far seemed very distant, a story.

But he'd come of his own choice, to make the hangings stop. The crowds were scattered again, back in their houses and shops, shipyards, and factories. Beth and the doctor and Xeno would return to the things that filled their days before Jack had run away from home so much farther than he'd ever intended. Ever imagined.

Outside the door, the noise was louder, and Jack could hear a voice that sounded like flint and fire. "Where is he?" it demanded. "Where is my son? Bring him to me at once!"

Jack stopped. She was talking about him. Arabella took his elbow to chivy him forward along the corridor to the top of the marble staircase.

"He is coming, Lady," said another voice, younger, a girl, perhaps one of the many who'd poked and prodded at him before he'd been taken to his room. "Any moment now."

Behave yourself, little Jack. Jack started and saw Lorcan standing half in shadow, his face a mask. *You have seen what I will do. Please her, or it will be your neck inside that noose.*

"H-how do you do that?" Jack asked him.

"Do what?" Arabella looked confused. "Oh! Sir Lorcan, didn't see you there. I'm taking him down right now."

"Of course." Lorcan spread his arms. "Do not let me keep you."

He didn't answer Jack.

The banister was cold beneath Jack's hand. He gripped it so his knuckles turned white as the marble. *Click, click.* His heels struck the stairs, counting the steps. At the bottom, Arabella steered him left, through the wide entrance hall and to another set of doors, opposite the ones he'd been through earlier. A footman stood ready. Jack felt his stare like hands on his face.

The doors opened onto a most beautiful room, but Jack had little chance for more than a brief impression of silk and brass and velvet.

This, then, must be the Lady, and she was the prettiest thing Jack had ever seen, so pretty it frightened him. She bloomed like an enormous red flower in the middle of the floor, her smile showing too many teeth. Her lips were very red, too, and her eyes a perfect blue. A small hat, ringed with diamonds, sat on her head.

"Splendid," she breathed, her eyes wide. "Oh, so very splendid."

She came closer. "Tell me your name."

"J-Jack," he said. His knees knocked together in the fancy breeches.

"Jack," she repeated. "A strong name. A *good* name."

It was my grandfather's, Jack wanted to say, but something whispered to him that this wouldn't be wise. So he said nothing at all.

"We are going to have such *fun*, Jack." She clapped her hands. "Parties and cake and all manner of smashing times. Are you pleased with your chambers? Are they good enough for you?"

Oddly, it felt to Jack that she was genuinely concerned about this. "Yes," he answered. "Thank you." *He hanged people to get me here.*

"So polite. Lovely."

She embraced him then, all perfume and powder. He thought of his mother, though he didn't know why. Certainly she'd never hugged him thus, or not for as long as Jack could remember. And then of Mrs. Pond, who'd always greeted him home from school, squeezing the very breath from him. He stood very still until the Lady released him.

"Splendid," she said once more.

"W-what do I call you?" Jack asked.

She blinked in surprise. "Why, Mother, of course."

Jack looked more closely at the room. A throne sat in the middle on a large rug, and curtains billowed at the windows. A girl was crouched, sweeping up shards of china. Portraits lined the walls, as they did in the corridor upstairs.

All were of boys who could pass for Jack's brothers, had he any, the oils faded and cracked, some more than others. Dozens of them. Even the newest appeared old, and though they all looked similar, Jack could tell that one was Lorcan, himself appearing like a slightly older version of Jack.

Jack looked, and thought of the brilliant white stone at the base of the tower, and tried to ignore the ache in his chest that wasn't caused by filthy air this time, but by knowing he would never be home again.

Preparations were made.

A great parade, decreed the Lady. The people would know of her new son. Another throne, a miniature of the one already in the grand room, was fetched, and Jack was forced to sit in it for hours on end as people came for her approval with fabrics to touch, food to sample.

And then she would send them all away, even the ladies-in-waiting, and it would just be her and Jack surrounded by the splendor and the portraits. He was allowed to play as much as he liked with the Tune-Turner, even to take it apart and put it together again for her amusement.

"Sir Lorcan of Havelock, Lady," announced the footman from the door. Jack raised his head. The Lady beckoned Lorcan forward.

"Ah, Lorcan, what news?" she asked. It was so quick

Jack was certain he'd imagined the flinch, the curling of Lorcan's hands, but then he was bowing, and when he straightened again, he was perfectly at ease.

"The fleets are in excellent repair, Lady," he said. "Ready to fly at your command."

Jack remembered the airships carving the sky over the park. Had Beth stayed with Dr. Snailwater, or had she returned to her birdcage gazebo to watch the passersby, now that Jack was gone?

The Lady smiled. "Excellent. All that must wait, however. We must celebrate first!"

"Do you think delaying is wise, Lady? The longer we wait, the stronger the colonies grow, more fond of their independence," said Lorcan.

This time, Jack was certain he saw anger. The Lady's eyes flashed as she half rose from her throne, but she glanced toward Jack and lowered herself again. "I do. Now leave us. Go inspect the palanquins, if you like. We are playing chess." A cat's smile curled her lips. "Send someone in with cake on your way."

Lorcan's heels tapped loudly over the floor. *You will grow old,* he said in Jack's head as he left. *Grow old and die in misery like all who came before me, but I will still be here. I have served her these two hundred years, and will an eternity more. Enjoy her favor while you can.*

A servant entered with a tray laden with tea and crumpets and cakes of different flavors. Lemon, strawberry jam, Battenberg with its thick layer of almond paste all around. The Lady moved a pawn. Arabella and the other girls, whose names Jack could not for the life of him remember, sat on the floor, whispering among themselves. Jack could see he would win, if only he moved his bishop this way, queen that.

He chose a knight.

"Well done, Lady," said Arabella, her gleaming eyes on Jack as he lay down his king. He looked away. But the Lady didn't seem to know he'd lost on purpose, that he had some notion of what would happen were he to anger her. She patted his head and motioned for a girl to pour the tea.

"What would you like to do next, dearest?" asked the Lady.

He wanted to explore the palace. Thus far, he'd really only seen his room, and this one, and the route between the two. Even the room to which he'd been led upon his arrival had been closed to him since.

Rings of silver and gold dug into his hand as she led him out, ordering Arabella and the footman not to follow. They would be perfectly fine on their own, she said. Together they wandered long corridors, into empty rooms he was told were used by dignitaries from foreign lands when they came to visit.

Jack couldn't help but notice they were filmed with a thin sheen of dust.

She took him to the library of which Beth had spoken, and he pretended surprise at its shelves reaching to the high ceilings. "Read anything you wish," she said. He thought of the books in his room at home.

But he liked it here. No school to be sent off to, and not once had the Lady sent him away so she might giggle with her friends in private. The throne room doors were not locked to him at any hour, and he wasn't reduced to peering through the keyhole at silly magic tricks.

Lorcan's, though, had not seemed so very silly. With his magic, Lorcan had power over life or death, killing the daisy, making the bird-shaped hairpin flutter as if it were real.

"Have you always lived here?" asked Jack. There were other palaces in his London; everything else seemed the same.

"For longer than you can imagine."

She's not like the rest of us. No one knows from whence she came, the doctor had said.

For a moment, Jack felt sorry for her, if that was really true. Whatever she was, she was lonely. Why else had she so desperately wanted a child?

He would be a good son to her. And she would be a good mother to him.

"Thank you for the dragon," he said. "I like to watch it fly."

"They always say that in the beginning," she whispered. Jack strained to hear her, and she stepped away to the window. "So grateful in the beginning, but they grow, and they must leave."

Jack was silent. Lorcan hadn't left, but he had grown older, at least for a while. And then he had . . . stopped.

The Lady clapped her hands. "Enough!" she said, wearing a merry expression once more. "Such fun we'll have! Come along, now."

There were no bedtimes, no bells to rouse him in the morning, though the clock tower was nearby and loud enough that it often did pull Jack from his dreams. Meals were served at a long table under gas chandeliers, or else the Lady had them brought to the thrones.

Beth was right. She was not so very terrible. Not terrible at all, in fact.

She loved him and showered him with gifts. New boots, sending for the cobbler the moment he complained that his pinched his toes, suits in his favorite colors, a small top hat when he happened to mention it.

The day of the parade approached. More people with their glass eyes or metal hands or rattling lungs bowed their entries and begged for the Lady's yea or nay. Jack sat in his chair and waited for them to be gone. Or, if he grew tired there, he would slip from the room to explore.

By far his favorite part of the palace was not, technically, *in* the palace. Through a room that seemed to exist because there's only so much hallway possible before a room is needed to break up the boredom, wide doors led to a courtyard. Enormous clockwork fans branched overhead like trees, so the air below was clean and fresh, nothing like the outdoors in the rest of the city. Faeries frolicked there, climbing the trees to drop to the flower beds, crushing them, or making faery foot dents in the soft grass.

It was here Arabella found him, her hair streaming behind as she ran. "Your lordship!" she called, tripping along the path that wound around the shrubbery. "You must come. You simply must!"

He followed her, through the pointless room, along the thick carpets and over the echoing marble. Behind the closed doors at the footman's back, Jack heard screams and an almighty crash.

The footman stepped aside. Jack swallowed, and Arabella nudged him.

"Why is she angry?" he asked. Something else broke, ringing out.

"Who can tell? Go." She nudged him again.

Slowly, Jack pushed open the door. He ducked. A vase struck the wall above his head, a glittering shower of crystal raining down, a drop slashing at his cheek.

"Where were you?" the Lady screamed. "You left!" Her face was red, lips smeared, hair a wild, wild tangle.

Inside his new leather boots, Jack's feet shook. "I—I didn't. I went to see the courtyard."

"You will never leave," she hissed. A dark thing curled in Jack's belly.

Never, never leave.

He took a deep breath, a step toward her. *Little boys do not cry*, said Mrs. Pond's kindly voice in his head. *Little boys are brave and do the things they must.* "I won't," he promised. "I won't leave, Mother."

CHAPTER FOURTEEN

Dragon Meets Dirigible

ON THE MORNING OF THE parade, Arabella shook Jack awake. She'd opened the curtains, though with the heavy clouds of soot and fug that lay over the city, it was never possible to tell whether, above them, the sun shone; it was brighter than dream darkness.

He blinked and pushed aside the coverlet, sliding from the high bed to the floor, bare toes wriggling in the carpet. Beyond the window, Londinium rose from the ashes of night, lamps flaring to life. If he squinted, he could see the guards patrolling the streets before the palace, feathers in their hats ruffled by breezes.

Jack's stomach fluttered, empty, hot. The parade.

Where he would look out at all the people and . . .

"Where do they think I come from?" he asked.

A collar fell from Arabella's hand. She bent to retrieve it. "Beg pardon, your lordship?"

"All of the . . . the subjects. I'm not like them. They'll see that." It was why Dr. Snailwater had disguised him, but he decided not to mention that to Arabella, who busied herself rummaging in a drawer.

"Same place as the Lady does, I 'spect," she said.

"And where's that?"

Arabella turned, leaned against the chest of drawers, and crossed her arms over herself. "Some things are so very old, it's as if they've been there forever. The Lady does me well, saved me from life on the docks, freezing me fingers off gutting fish all day long, and I can handle her temper. Poking my nose in where it's got no business won't do me no favors."

"But I'm not as old as her."

Arabella shrugged. "They'll think you are. They don't ask questions, neither. Not where a body can hear them, anyways."

He dressed in the suit she gave him. Green today, green as forests and faery eyes, and this time he did look in the mirror. Everything about him shone new and bright. The day before, the Lady had sent for a barber, who'd snipped away at Jack's hair until it was a smooth cap. Dark locks curled on the floor and had stuck to his shoes.

Outside, the clock chimed. Inside, the palace thrummed, a heartbeat of footsteps and orders and *oh-blast-mustn't-forget-to's*. The maids, serfs, guards, and ladies-in-waiting stepped out of his way as he crossed the marble, past the footman, into the throne room.

She was simply too beautiful to be real. The choosing of Jack's suit was no mistake, for she wore green, too, a deep velvet strung through and through with sparkling emeralds. A facry scampered out from behind her gown, cackling as it ran beneath a sideboard, and she did not even kick it, so wide was her red, red smile. A topper crowned with peacock feathers sat on her head. From it hung a veil, fine as mist over her eyes, down to the curve of her cheeks.

"Mother," he said.

Her smile grew further still. "Darling Jack. Come to me."

One each day until you come to me. He pushed the thought away as one would a distasteful food. That had been Lorcan, not her. She wrapped her arms around him, tight enough to crease his collar.

Breakfast was laid out, deviled eggs and kippers, peaches in cream and pastries filled with jam. Jack wished for porridge, thin and watery the way he liked it, but chased an egg around his plate while people bustled in and out. The noise from the street reached in to touch the palace with excited fingers. His throat stuck together so he could not even swallow tea.

The Lady didn't notice, too occupied with giving orders and clapping at the smallest perfections.

"I have the most marvelous surprise for you," she announced. "We are— Oh, Lorcan." Her smile turned brittle as bones as he entered the room. Jack looked away. "Is it ready?"

"There was a matter to attend to, Lady," said Lorcan. His eyes glittered. Not red, this time, but Jack remembered. "It is ready."

"Come along, darling," she said. Lorcan gave a funny kind of jerk. The Lady reached for Jack's hand, and Jack did not miss Lorcan's scowl. Guards fell into step behind, following their journey through the palace to a set of high doors leading to a courtyard.

Jack clasped his hand over his mouth to keep from gasping. An airship hovered a few feet from the ground, taking up nearly the entire courtyard, end to end. Its hull was smooth, sleek, never scraped by rocks or crusted with barnacles. He craned his head to see the masts strung with sails and flying flags of crimson edged with gold. Guards ran about the deck, plumes whipped in the wind, shouting to one another for ropes.

"The palanquins seemed far too ordinary," said the Lady, delighted. "Now everyone will see you! Isn't it splendid?"

It *was*.

Beside him, Jack heard Lorcan huff, but he did not care. *He* was the Lady's son now, and if she wanted him to ride in a boat grander than any he'd seen on the Thames, carving through a sea of air, he wasn't bothered by what Lorcan thought of the matter.

"May we go aboard, Mother?" There wasn't the slightest pang at the word, for she was his mother now, and let him do all manner of things his own never allowed, and she didn't fly into a rage at him, because he could eat the cakes Beth never could.

Beth. He did miss her, a little bit. No doubt she was skipping through the streets or sheltered in her birdcage. Perhaps she'd come to the parade. He'd catch a glimpse and wave at her.

"Of course, my dearest. The gangway, if you please, Lorcan. Arabella, do try not to slouch."

Lorcan signaled to a guard on the deck, and as if the ship were a sea monster itself, a great mouth opened in the bottom, ready to swallow them whole. Slowly, the ramp descended, finally stopping an inch from the cobbles. The Lady held tightly to Jack's hand as she led him up into the belly, full of clangs and thumps and that same thunderous rumbling Jack had heard on his first sight of the ships. So much louder now. The floor shook. Jack's teeth rattled, and it was difficult to keep his eyes open.

But he wriggled free of the Lady's grasp and moved toward the roar. Too late, it occurred to him that this might displease her, but when he looked back she was smiling. It was Lorcan whose face looked like the business edge of a blade.

Jack didn't wish to wonder, just then, why Lorcan had gone to such trouble to bring him here only to hate him. There was too much to look at: the spiral staircase that led up to the deck, folded sails and coiled ropes, darkened shadows where guards lurked ready to be called upon. Rows of cannons along either side, their barrels lined up perfectly with holes cut into the sides of the ship.

Most of all, the open door beside the stairs, the maddeningly incomplete glimpses of the engine in the room beyond. He ran to it, through it, engulfed by the sound. It was like nothing Jack had ever seen. The enormity of it, the clouds of steam thick enough to blanket the whole sky, sucked from the room by a shaft that led upward. Every metal part, tiny and huge, playing its well-oiled part. Spinning, hissing, churning.

Fingers clasped his forearm. Jack looked up. Lorcan glared at him in return, dragging him roughly from the engine room. "Careful near that steam, child," said Lorcan as they went. "How sad it would be if you were to get . . . hurt."

The instant they were in sight of the Lady, Lorcan's grip loosened and his mouth slackened into what might generously be termed a smile.

"Go on," he ordered Jack. The Lady went first, the liquid green silk of her dress melting improbably upward on the stairs.

The deck was nearly grander still than the inside of the ship, if not as interesting. Sails snapped in frustration against the masts that rose high above the deck. A huge wheel bloomed at the helm, beside . . . Surely there wasn't always a parlor set out here. This was to please the Lady, but there it was, right at the front. Two thrones, one large, one smaller, sat atop a finely spun rug. Little tables sat spindly-legged as insects holding dishes of sweets and cakes on their backs. There was even a Tune-Turner, but Jack doubted he would ask for music. And a chessboard.

Arabella helped the Lady to her chair, which faced out to the palace, level with the windows on the highest floor.

So that they could see the crowds, Jack realized, and wave to them.

"Sit, Jack."

"Yes, Mother."

"Cake?"

It was barely an hour since the breakfast he hadn't

eaten. He took one and held it, crumbs crawling over his fingers as guards rushed to and fro around them, never setting foot on the rug. Arabella curled on the rug as she did inside the palace. Lorcan was nowhere to be seen without Jack craning his neck. He didn't.

The ship gave a great shudder. A rope whistled through the air and they jolted upward. The palace windows were at Jack's knees now, then the deck, then he had to lean over the railing. The palace roof spiked and sloped below. He looked across to the far end where the clock tower stood, its faces shrouded in a black veil.

There had been no rain.

The tops of the masts carved etchings in the swathe of cloud. Jack held fast to the arms of his throne as the ship turned away from the curving arm of the river and away from the palace.

"Going down!" someone called. Jack's stomach leaped, but the descent was smooth, controlled to an inch. No motorcars or carriages barred their way on the streets that, he saw now, were lined with people. Hands and eyes caught the light in diamond sparks. The crowd wasn't as noisy as it had been for the hangings, but then, for the hangings they had known precisely what they were coming to see. Curiosity painted every face. Necks bent to see as the ship skimmed the cobbles and the people saw first the Lady, then Jack.

"'S'never a boy!" shouted a man from somewhere in the mass.

"'T'is!" replied another.

Voices rustled; Jack strained to hear them. What did they think of him? Where did they think he'd come from? Despite what Arabella said, they must think *something*, and if it was that he'd appeared from the same place as their Lady, well, where was that?

"Oh, they love you!" cried the Lady.

It was impossible to linger on any one face for long. The enormous airship slid through the streets, along the edge of the park where Jack had found Beth. He jumped from the chair to lean over the railing, looking for her. Anything—a flicker of hair ribbon, Dr. Snailwater's fluffy white hair, because where one was, the other would be.

No luck. His heart sank, just a bit. Possibly they were angry with him for leaving, though he had explained everything he could in the note. Everything but Lorcan's voice, which only made him sound mad.

From the corner of his eye, Jack saw Lorcan watching him and smiling for once.

Enjoy it while you can, your lordship. Jack shook his head to clear the voice, which was dripping with nastiness.

The crowd swelled and was now a seething of flags on little sticks. Beside him, the Lady's thrill was warm and thick as wool. She waved now and then before sitting back and commanding Arabella to fetch some tea.

Jack grinned. Parades and flags and cheers and this magnificent place where everything ran on clockwork and steam under the rule of his new mother.

It was all for him.

Slowly, the crowd thinned as the ship sailed through the city's widest streets. Far behind them, people were likely going back to their measured, clicking lives, small gears turning big ones, the cogs of the Empire continuing to run.

"Back to the palace," Lorcan ordered a guard at the helm, but the Lady held up her hand.

"It's so lovely to be out," she said. "A tour, I think! Yes, Jack should see the country."

"Lady—"

Her eyes turned to flint. "It was not a request."

She will spoil you now, little Jack, but you won't be young forever.

Jack ignored Lorcan. Inside, his heart lifted with the ship rising into the air. Lorcan's boots rang on the deck, storming away until Jack couldn't hear them over the engine. The tea Arabella brought grew cold; the rooftops shrank.

At speed, it took only moments to reach the outskirts of the city. Towering smokestacks sat in fields and hurled blackness to the skies. The ship wove around them, turning deftly this way and that with the help of flapping sails and lucky winds.

In the distance, if he squinted, Jack saw what he was certain was sunlight striping a patchwork of green. He took a deep breath and coughed; the air was no cleaner, not yet. When he rubbed his eyes, his hand came away smudged with soot.

"Come sit with me, darling," said the Lady. "I wish to tell you a story. Arabella, go amuse yourself elsewhere."

Jack wanted to look, not listen, but he thought of her tone when she'd spoken to Lorcan, and so he turned away from the railing and took his seat. She was turning her china teacup in her delicate hands. The wind had tossed the feathers on her little topper, and her skin was perhaps a bit gray with ash, but she was still beautiful. She smiled at him.

"They all know you now," she said. Then, to herself, "It never lasts long."

"What do you mean, Mother?"

The teacup turned a half circle. "You will grow old. It happens so quickly."

Something fluttered in Jack's belly. "You don't get older."

The Lady shook her head. "Occasionally I think that would be grand, but no, I will never be anything except what I am now."

"How?" Jack swallowed. "How is that possible . . . Mother?" He was aware that the voices around them had ceased, or perhaps it was only that they faded away so that he could properly listen.

"I am rather special, my darling. I mean, clearly." Her laugh tinkled, drifted away on the wind like chimes, and she began to speak in earnest. "The place you come from, London, is a bit different, isn't it? Lorcan tells me stories after those times when he must visit. I haven't seen it in a very long time, and so he has created this one for me to look just like it is now—bridges and buildings and that magnificent clock!—so that I can know, but it is still different.

"This land"—she took a hand from her cup and waved it in the direction of the mountains in the distance, snow-capped, edges crisp as silence—"has ever been an island particularly receptive to faery magic. To gods and monsters."

Jack couldn't breathe, but it wasn't because of filthy air. The clouds had thinned, cleared as they left the city behind. Frosty blue, lit by the sun, stretched out as far as Jack could see.

The Lady gaily threw her hands upward. "Oh, I do not know exactly how it all works. Only that there is this, and your land, and perhaps a hundred others. We can never be certain of the number. All a bit the same and a bit not."

That was what Xeno had said, too. That there might be worlds that ran on water or sunlight or other things, unknown things.

"There are doorways between these worlds; you must simply know where to look. Oh, yes, the signs are always clear. I went through only once, long ago, in the hopes of taking your land for myself. The errors of others cursed me." She scowled, her face ugly for an instant. "Tell me, little Jack, is perfection too much to ask for?"

He did not know what to say. The mountains were nearly upon them.

"I tell you, it is not. I brought back as many of your people as I could, but their children were not perfect, their grand-children less so. They are weak and stupid; the clouds sicken them. And so Lorcan went through the doorway to fetch you for me, as the one before fetched him, and now we can have an excellent good time while you are still young. Someday, after you are old, it will be your turn to fetch me another son, but let's not think of that just now."

Slowly, Jack turned to peer around the back of the throne. Lorcan was ten yards away. Watching.

She didn't know.

Tell her I have destroyed the doorway, said Lorcan inside Jack's head, *and you will not make it off this ship alive.*

"What would you like to do while you are young, dearest?"

Jack stood, feeling taller than Lorcan. Now he had a secret of his own. "May I steer the ship?"

The captain was called, Jack's hands placed on the great wheel. Lorcan's eyes burned on Jack as if someone had dropped two hot coals down his coat. The Lady clapped, all gleaming joy.

Jack laughed into the wind that rushed his face, filled his ears with a howl. The mountains swallowed them, a forest of stone. He turned the ship so sharply a tray of cakes clattered to the rug, a grotesque smash of raspberries and cream. A bird swooped ahead, wings bent at the hinges to catch the air. A stream tumbled below, white and frothed. The wheel fit perfectly to his fingers; the ship seemed to answer his thoughts. This way, then that.

It came from nowhere. At first, Jack thought the roar was only the wind and the engine. Behind him, men screamed to be heard.

"Ready the cannons!"

Jack spun. Nearly fell in surprise. A jet of steam, boiling, scalding, blew from the dragon's mouth. Warmth brushed Jack's arms. Wings half as long as the ship itself screeched, in desperate need of oiling. Great bronze scales covered it all over. Glass eyes large as boulders swept back and forth over the running men. It was just like his small one at the palace, but exponentially, terrifyingly larger.

"Give me the wheel," ordered the captain.

But Jack held fast.

"Don't kill it!" he said. "Please."

The Lady's hand was over her mouth, and Jack thought, fleetingly, that she was hiding a smile.

More steam, a blade of it keen enough to slice a sail in two. The cloth whipped away to the mountains and beyond into nothing. "The cannons!" Lorcan shouted. Jack turned the wheel, sending a chase of teapots and sugar tongs across the deck. A cannonball shot from below, missing the dragon's belly by a foot. A sheet of rock fell to earth; a plume of fire rose from the mountainside. "Stupid child!"

The slap echoed around the ship, above the cacophony. Lorcan staggered into Jack's sight and out of it again, reeling from the Lady's blow as Jack urged the ship around the jagged mountain peaks.

"It's thirsty!" Jack shouted to the captain. "It only needs oil!" He was certain, certain that the dragon didn't want to harm them. It was frightened, caged by the entire sky.

The ship canted and spun in the wake of the dragon's wings. Jack's knuckles were white against the brass wheel, holding tight as he could as he tried to dodge the angry gusts of steam and the frantic, flapping creature. Men

skittered over the deck, running to and fro. Arabella cowered against a mast. The Lady, fearless, sat on her throne. Lorcan was nowhere to be seen.

"Take her up!" the captain yelled, muscles straining, an oil drum hoisted in his arms. Two guards stood behind him, struggling to keep a grip on their own heavy containers.

With a whoosh, the ship rose, fifty feet, a hundred. Jack's stomach dropped into his boots. The dragon roared and steamed, furious, twisting its body to aim for the dirigible.

Before it could, the captain tipped the oil over the side, a rippling black ribbon the dragon caught and swallowed like a magic trick. It drank and drank until the drum was dry, then emptied the next, and the next. Flecks of oil spattered its eyes, its snout. But its great metal body shuddered and seemed to calm, wings almost lazy with content, swooping and drifting away from the ship and past the next peak until it was gone.

Jack peeled his fingers from the wheel. They were shaking. He looked at the Lady, who was most definitely smiling now. She wasn't afraid because she couldn't die, he thought, and Jack himself had never felt quite so alive. He smiled into the wind.

CHAPTER FIFTEEN

The Other Doorway

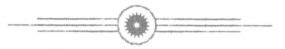

THE PALACE WAS SILENT, AS well it should be. Chimes marking an hour past midnight had rung out from the great clock ten minutes earlier. Jack sat at his window, wide awake, for it had been a very exciting day, what with the dragon and the airship and learning about Mother.

She hadn't told him everything, he was certain, but there was time enough for that later. He would be her last son, though she did not know it yet, the last of the perfect children brought through the doorway to live in this marvelous world.

Marvelous . . . for the moment. And if he didn't peer too closely down to the street, where people gasped and wheezed through their grilles and metal lungs, hobbled on feet in desperate need of oiling.

Where people were hanged.

Inside the palace it was marvelous. His dragon, which now seemed positively tiny in comparison to the enormous one of the mountains, flapped above, its belly full, its snorts ones of lazy contentment. *Harleye Street was a bit marvelous, too,* he thought, pressing his nose to the glass to see if he could spot it, out there in the maze of homes and factories, asleep beneath a blanket of soot.

Bang.

Jack jumped, turned to look around the room, but everything was in place, quiet. Ears strained, he listened for noises beyond the door, but nothing came.

Scrape.

"H-hello?"

There was no answer. Lorcan's pointed face flashed through Jack's mind, scowling and mean. Only it was not Lorcan who appeared suddenly in the hearth, stepping carefully around coals that had cooled hours since.

"Beth!"

"'Lo, Jack," she said, hopping out onto the carpet. Jack wasn't sure where to look first—at her, or the door just shut behind her, seamless and invisible in the smoke-blackened brick.

"What are you doing here?" he asked, surprise making him sound rude when he didn't mean to. "Is that a secret passageway?"

"The doctor expressly forbade me to come, which gave me the idea," said Beth, hopping neatly up to perch on the edge of Jack's bed. "Got a barrow boy to wind me up so's I could stay awake. Them passageways are all over the palace, if you know where to look, and I always had lots of time to explore when the Lady was having one of her wee fits. There's a few spots in and out. Might've bent a hinge squeezing in," she finished, inspecting a finger.

"The doctor told you not to?" Jack frowned.

"Wasn't best pleased that you'd run off in the middle of the night, even if you did leave a note," Beth said with a shrug. "He'll calm down soon enough. We saw you at the parade, all fancy on the ship."

So they *had* been there. Jack relaxed and grinned at Beth. Now that she was here, he knew he'd missed her a great deal more than he'd wanted to admit to himself, and could not admit to Mother or Lorcan or even Arabella. "Show me," he said, pointing to the hearth.

"Look at you, ordering people about already." But there was no malice in Beth's words, merely her usual easy good nature. "Come on, then, and bring that lamp."

It was difficult to keep from laughing as they stepped

into the darkness and ran, Jack keeping a close eye on
Beth's heels, flashing in the lamplight, the flame dancing
within the glass. The thick stone made everything cold and
musty. Something with a dozen pin-sharp legs landed on
Jack's cheek, and he heard the metal clatter on the ground
when he brushed it away. Beth turned abruptly to the left,
forcing Jack to throw his free hand out so as not to crash
into the wall ahead.

She took him first to the room that had been hers, a
froth of roses and frills coated with dust. Blank-eyed dolls
stared from atop the chest of drawers, an empty cage, white
and lacy and not large enough for a dragon hung from a
brass stand. Jack could tell, as soon as they walked in, that
Beth didn't much like the room, but it made him think of
a thing that hadn't occurred to him before.

"Why did Dr. Snailwater make you a girl?"

"What do you mean?"

"All the children fetched from where I come from were
boys, sons. But you're a girl. The doctor said all the others
he made were girls." And there were no portraits of them
hanging downstairs on the wall. Perhaps Mother didn't
think there needed to be, seeing as Beth and her sisters
weren't quite the same as people.

"Oh." Beth came closer. "I'm not s'posed to know, you
know, but I heard them talking about it, last time Sir

Lorcan came to Harleye Street. Was, let's see, a few years ago now, and the Lady'd just sent me away, so I went back to the doctor. Sir Lorcan came in a right foul mood, as if he's ever in anything else. Said we were no good, should all be smashed to bits."

Jack swallowed. He remembered that the doctor had never told Beth this was, indeed, how the others had ended up.

"At any rate," she continued, "the doctor offered to try his hand at making a boy, and Lorcan, if you'll hark it, got even angrier. Started tossing things around the workshop like a madman. Said *he* was the Lady's son and wouldn't have another. Though he was wrong, 'course, seeing as now there's you."

Yes, now there was Jack. And Lorcan despised him.

"Want to see my very favorite room in the whole palace?" Beth asked, smiling brightly. Jack nodded.

It was a long trip, what felt like the length of the place and back again. Up staircases like ladders, down until Jack thought he felt the rumble of trains underneath the earth. Beth stopped at a stretch of wall that looked no different from any other in the small pool of flickering light from the lamp he held. She pushed at it, and it opened onto a dark room, its size obvious even then. A ballroom, at least, their every motion echoing. Jack raised the light and gasped.

The room was very cold, and this was strange. It felt as if it should be warm, hot, aglow as it was with gold like fire. Everything in it shone like the sun that was so rare here, as if that was part of the Empire's magic—the sun itself pulled from the sky and trapped within these walls. Of course that was not the case, but Jack felt he couldn't be blamed for thinking so.

Drapes of golden silk shot through with crimson blocked the windows. Paintings in gilded frames hung on the walls, the canvases within stained all the colors of flame. A thicket of pedestals filled the room, polished, shining statues of birds perched on each one. Some were in full flight, wings spread, others skeletal and hunched, still more staid and watchful as gargoyles, caught mid-leer by the sculptor.

If *sculptor* was indeed the right word. Jack supposed it must be, but these creatures were built, not molded. Assembled from bits and pieces of other things—a bronze gear here, a flat, hammered feather there. Like his dragon, only these were not alive, and didn't feel as if they ever had been.

"Isn't it beautiful?" Beth asked, her voice a whisper that bounced off every surface.

"What is it? Why are these hidden away?"

Beth began to move among the statues, touching one

now and then with her bent finger. "'Spect someone thinks they'll be nicked. Safer in here. They used to be out in the city, just regular old statues, see?" She led him to one of the large paintings, cracked with age, the oils glimmering in the lamplight. It was the birdcage in which he'd first spotted Beth herself; one of the great gold birds was set precisely where Beth had stood that day.

"Why is this bird everywhere?" Jack asked. And it was, not simply in this room, but everywhere. The handle on the walking stick of that old man, weeks ago. Outside public houses and in the crystal ball.

"I'm not the best one to tell the story," Beth said. "Xeno, he's your man for that. Knows it better'n anyone."

"What story?" But Jack thought he knew—it was the story the doctor had insisted was a myth, stopped Xeno from telling Jack. He moved to the next painting. Here the bird was soaring above the clouds, a burning ball shooting through the sky. "What is the *Flight of Fire?*" he asked, reading a small brass plaque affixed to the frame.

"It's—What was that?"

Footsteps. Not in the passageway, but out in the corridor and coming closer. Almost instantly Beth was at Jack's side, strong fingers pinching his arm as she pulled him behind the nearest curtain to hide in the folds. The window glass chilled his back, but he didn't move, used his last breath to blow out the lamp and then held it as a key turned in the lock.

Jack peered through a crack in the cloth. Lorcan's neat shoes clicked slowly across the floor, a lamp of his own held aloft. Closer, he came, closer until Jack was sure Lorcan was following the sound of Jack's own heart, its impossibly loud *thump* a beacon straight to the curtain.

But this was not the case. Lorcan stopped at the very painting that had caught Jack's attention seconds before, and for what seemed an eternity he simply gazed at it. Finally, he nodded to himself, turning away. Jack took Beth's strange, hinged hand with his own decidedly clammy one, a sigh of relief escaping his chest.

Lorcan spun around, eyes on the curtains. Blood rushed in Jack's ears, and he was home again, home kneeling on the floor, peering through the keyhole. Lorcan's eyes caught the light of the lamp he held, flashing red as they had done all that time ago, when Jack had been so certain Lorcan knew he was there, spying on his mother and her friends.

But the worst that could have happened then was a hiding, perhaps being sent to his room with no supper. Jack did not want to think of what the worst Lorcan might do could be. He held his breath, tried to make himself invisible behind the heavy cloth, wished Beth to be less solid and real. Dizzied, Jack almost couldn't believe it when Lorcan retreated, a brief shaft of light falling in from the corridor before the lock clicked shut.

"Wait," Beth whispered, hardly more than a breath. After several minutes it seemed as if he was truly gone and they edged out from behind the silk and made their way to the secret door. Back along the passageways, twisting left and right, up steep staircases and down others they ran.

Jack's chamber was terribly dull after the bright, rich gold. They fell through the hearth, the dragon screeching at their sudden arrival. "Shush," Jack told it, chest aching for air. Beyond the windows, it was nearly morning, the entire night gone in a maze of adventure that felt harmless now that they were safe and warm and away from Lorcan.

"I should be off," Beth said. "Are you coming?"

Jack started. He could, couldn't he? Simply flee with Beth and never look back.

But the doorway was gone; he couldn't return to London, and Mother—his mother *here*—needed him. She would have no more sons. In the calm of this room, Lorcan wasn't frightening. He could do nothing to Jack, so long as Jack kept his secret.

"I like it here," he told Beth. The truth, near enough.

Beth nodded. "The doctor will worry if I don't pop in

for a hello soon. I'll come back to see you, though, if you like."

"Yes, please."

She slipped back behind the hidden door, and Jack climbed into his bed to wait for Arabella to wake him for breakfast.

CHAPTER SIXTEEN

The Accident That Wasn't

WHEN LORCAN DID HIS MAGIC—*part* of his magic—he did so alone. It was a private matter, after all. Those who wanted to learn would not do so from him. They could find their own faery teachers, teachers who knew magic as old as the hills, and tear their metal bodies apart if they refused, just as he had done.

There were no parlor tricks here. Only a fool wouldn't wish to know one's enemy.

The copper bowl was already laid out, ashes dusting the bottom, a square of purple silk, exactly four sprigs of thyme. A small amount of water, not the filthy muck from the Thames but a vial from a hidden spring in the mountains. A lock of hair. Jack Foster's hair.

A week, the boy had been unsupervised in the Empire of Clouds for a week, getting up to who knew what kind of mischief, and the oddity had visited him at the palace the previous night. He had seen her leaving, trotting away through the streets in early dawn.

But Lorcan could know, if not what she had told him then, at least what the boy had done in the time before this hair was cut. He could discover whether anyone had told the boy the story.

"Trinket," he said very quietly. The imp appeared from nowhere. It rattled as it shook.

"M-Master?" it said.

"You know what I require," said Lorcan. The imp took in the objects on the desk.

"I am near empty, sir." It trembled harder.

Lorcan raised his eyebrows and passed the faery a pair of shears, strong enough to cut through metal. It climbed on the desk, its foot catching once again a spot on the edge where a groove had been worn by many occasions such as this. It closed its eyes and latched the shears around a finger.

It was not blood, not precisely. Long ago, the creature had learned not to scream, so there was only a tinny squeak to mark the snap, the clunk of metal on wood as the finger fell, the greasy hiss as the dark liquid poured into the copper bowl. The first gush splattered against the bottom, then faded to a dribble. *Drip. Drip. Drip.*

"Enough," said Lorcan. It wouldn't do to drain the thing completely. "Go now, but stay close. I will need you again before long."

The imp moved, irritatingly slowly, gathering its finger and dropping to the floor. A moment later it was gone the same way it had come, presumably off to the metallurgists now to be patched up, but this was not Lorcan's concern.

He needed to see.

Onto the oil he dropped the herbs, green against brown. Lamplight shimmered and danced. The water, now, to sit on top, trapping the thyme inside, and then the hair, scattered like dark feathers. He covered the bowl with the silk and waited, ears pricked, a sparkmaker held in his hand. The timing must be exact. A breeze, thick, cloying, oozed in the open window. Lorcan wrinkled his nose, but he had to hear.

He knew an instant before the great clock tower chimed midnight. A breath, and then the first ring of the bell. The silk dropped to the floor. The bowl rippled. His thumb flicked against the sparkmaker's wheel.

A column of fire, red and gold and scented with thyme,

rose from the bowl, the flames shaping into pictures.

There he was, the boy Jack. Lorcan's hands curled. How dare he be so like the Lady? How dare she love him so much, when it was Lorcan who had been the ideal son for more than two centuries? The boy was perfect even in his grubby clothes, fascination and confusion on his face as he stepped through the door. Taking in the streets, the strangeness.

Walking into the park.

The flames hissed, hit by the raindrops that sent the people running for cover for fear of rust and soaked the boy's shirt. He kept on, along the path to the gazebo, which was not empty.

Aha.

Lorcan watched another five minutes, everything he needed to see. It was all there. Satisfied, he stepped away. The boy had not discovered what kept Lorcan strong and whole, and this was Lorcan's only true fear. Everything else could be dealt with. The fire dropped until only a single flame skated around the bowl, and then it too was gone, leaving nothing save a small pile of ash, which would keep for the next time. Trinket brought him a cloth, with which he carefully wiped the traces of oil and soot from his hands, from the creases of his fingers and lines of his palms.

It was late, but that was all to the good. The strange creature had always let itself wind down at night when it lived in the palace. His guards came running at his call, left just as quickly with their instructions. That meddlesome doctor, with his unnatural experiments, was too useful to dispose of, but he could be taught a lesson. Oh, yes.

He did not have long to wait. The guards returned, Beth carried between them like a plank of wood. The ribbon loose from her hair, one shoe hanging precariously from its foot.

The window was still open, and Lorcan scarcely paused as he took her from the guards and carried her to the ledge.

It took only the smallest of pushes and she tumbled, turning over and over, dress billowed on the wind. She smashed in a storm of wires and gears on the courtyard below.

"Oh, dear," said Lorcan. And he smiled.

CHAPTER SEVENTEEN

The Win & the Loss

GRAY SNOW FELL UPON THE Empire, turned it to a charcoal rendering. Rounded and edgeless, the seam of one building smudged into the next.

Days had come to matter little, in the way a single grain of sand matters little to the beach. Each one was a sparkling, crystal thing that melted against the days before it. As Jack watched the city turn dull and soft from his window, he could remember only a few shining months of laughter, music, long games of chess by the fire. His portrait had been finished, and it hung on the wall with the others. Every now and then, the Lady would announce that she was bored, and they would take another flight in an airship, but Jack was glad not to meet any more dragons.

The tiny one in his room was enough to be getting on with.

Beth had not visited him again, but perhaps she would after the holidays. Several times, Jack had tried to explore the secret passages alone, but without Beth's help, he only got hopelessly lost. Not only had he not found a way out of the palace, but he hadn't even managed to find the rooms to which Beth had taken him, her own and the beautiful golden one with its paintings and birds. Although, remembering what happened there, it was likely best that Jack not go poking around again.

It would be Christmas soon. Piles of presents under a magnificent tree and plum puddings and glass baubles to catch the light. That was the way Mrs. Pond always did it, and Jack knew he had only to ask. His new mother would give him everything he wished.

In fact, he would go and ask right now. Arabella had tucked him into bed an hour before, but the palace was his to roam as he liked, even after bedtime. The Lady, especially, wouldn't be angry with him.

The marble was cold beneath his toes, tinged with some of the chill that frosted everything beyond his window. Jack padded down the stairs. Even the footmen and guards had gone to their beds; perhaps the Lady was in her own rooms, as well. But no, for there were voices coming from the throne room.

"I have already said no, Lorcan. Why must you continue to test me? You act as if I don't know your secrets, or wish me to keep them for you."

Jack crept closer to the closed door.

"I did it for you, Lady," Lorcan said. He sounded distraught, as Jack had never heard him. "Everything I have done, all for you."

The Lady laughed. "But I no longer need you. I have Jack."

Silence.

"He is too young to captain the fleets. Lady, if we simply give the colonies what they ask for—"

"Then everyone shall be happy!" she said. The unmistakable sound of her clapping pierced the wood against Jack's ear. "I like happy. I am far too pleased to go to war, Lorcan. I do not need those places across the seas. Let them rule themselves, and I will spend my time with my son."

"Andrasta—"

"It would upset Jack," she said, and he blinked at the sound of his name. "Think of how he saved the dragon. Such a good boy. Such a gentle boy. Such a *perfect* boy . . . and you wanted to kill the beast! He would not wish to go to war over a few handfuls of land. I have more than I could ever hope for right here, on this island. Let that be enough."

Another silence. Jack thought of the hangings. How

it had made him ill to imagine the swinging, the kicking feet. The last one, which he'd seen with Beth. Mother was right; he didn't want the Empire to be at war.

"Go, Lorcan. Do . . . whatever it is you do. Leave us to our fun. Inspect the fleets if you must, but you are not to command them into battle. We shall have peace." Her words sparked, hinting at a fire.

"As you like, Lady." Lorcan's voice was strung tight as a crossbow. Quick as his feet would take him, Jack ran to the nearest room and slipped into the shadow of a rather fine wardrobe, holding his breath until he heard Lorcan's boots fade far away. And waited another minute after that.

"Mother?" he said, stepping into the room.

She turned from the window, all bright smile and gleeful eyes. "Darling boy, what is it? Can you not sleep?"

He decided it was best to wait to ask about Christmas. "No," he said, and let her pet his hair and tell him a faery story—about real faeries—until a yawn threatened to crack his jaw. Even so, it was some time after he returned to bed that sleep found him. So, there would be no war. He was glad of this. Being a soldier was supposed to be a fine calling, but from what he knew, war seemed a silly thing. Boys got in trouble for fighting at school; it made Headmaster Adams shout and sometimes he'd whip them so they couldn't sit down for a week.

But this was not the most interesting thing to think about. *You act as if I don't know your secrets.* Curiosity burned inside Jack. It couldn't be that Lorcan was a magician; he'd made no secret of that, from the moment he'd rung the bell at the Fosters' home in London.

It was something else. Something, possibly, to do with the golden room, and Jack made up his mind to discover it.

Perhaps Lorcan had taken the Lady's advice and gone away, for he was nowhere to be found the next morning. Jack was glad of this, too. He set about doing all he could to put the Lady in the best possible mood, entertaining her by taking apart the Tune-Turner and putting it back together, asking for more cake, suggesting they amuse themselves with a favorite game of hiding in the palace, taking it in turns to find the other. Arabella and the other girls laughed, though they did not join in, and made sure hot tea was waiting when the fun ended.

Jack had discovered a great deal of the palace with this game, though not as much as Beth had known. There was an entire room filled with clocks, each wound to different times and ran at different speeds, so that it was never possible to tell if he'd been hiding for a minute or an hour. Another lined with mirrors, where if he stayed too long he nearly forgot which of him was the real one.

At the end of the afternoon, the Lady sat on her throne

and watched as Jack tinkered with the great machine that sucked the dust from the rugs, proud when it stopped making that irritating noise or coughing up puffs of soot.

"I wish to be alone with my mother," he said. Arabella gave him a startled look, but saw herself and the other girls from the room. The Lady smiled brilliantly as Jack went to sit at her feet, a cake, which he slowly pulled apart, in his hand.

"What makes Lorcan so special?" Jack asked.

The Lady blinked in surprise. "Darling! Has he upset you?" She began to rise from her throne, but Jack stopped her.

"No, Mother," he said, which was a lie, but she wouldn't know, or punish him for it if she did. "But if I knew how he stayed young, then I could do the same, and be with you forever."

"Oh." Her voice dropped to a whisper. "That isn't possible."

"Why, though? Why isn't it possible?"

Her fingers whitened, gripping the arms of her throne. "Because there was only ever one, and he destroyed it. He told me, and by then it was too late to punish him."

One *what*? Jack opened his mouth to ask, and the door opened, too.

Lorcan swept in, topper under his arm starred with snowflakes, hands coated in oil and ash. "Lady," he said, bowing deeply. "Might I borrow young Jack for a time? Your lordship," he said to Jack, bowing again. *Keep your smile and hold your tongue, little Jack. Do not make me do anything unfortunate. We are merely going to talk.*

"Of course," she said, distracted, gazing out the window. "Go and be the best of friends, but do not keep him from me long, Lorcan, or I shall miss him too much to bear."

"Indeed, Lady."

Jack followed Lorcan from the room, half running to keep up with the man's quick steps, reminded of when he had followed Lorcan to the clock. He hadn't the faintest idea what Lorcan wanted with him, but that was all right, since he knew what he wanted from Lorcan.

To find out what, exactly, Lorcan had destroyed.

A palace guard stood at the front door, ready to hold it for them as they ventured out. Jack hadn't left the palace on foot since his arrival. It was cold, and the wind made swirling ghosts of the snow. Jack shivered inside the thin clothes that were warm enough only for indoors.

Beyond gates crusted by icicles, a carriage waited in a puddle, blasting warmth several paces around. The driver jumped out to hold the door, just as Wilson did, but there were no horses here. Lorcan ushered Jack inside, waiting until he had settled on a wide bench before climbing in himself. A thick wall separated the compartment from the driver.

"We did not have the best of starts, you and I," Lorcan began. Slowly, the city began to slide past the windows.

Jack held his tongue.

"I, as anyone, must do what is necessary. This, you will learn. And what is necessary is the Lady's happiness. Without her, we would all be—" He let his fingers float through the air. "I was her son before you. Were you aware of this?"

"Yes," said Jack. They were crossing a bridge over the frozen river. Huge cracks ran through the ice, so that the whole thing looked like a spider's web.

"And now, now I am nothing. Not her child, merely the commander of an army she will have stay home, warm in their beds, instead of fighting for the Empire as is their duty. You will grow old, and I will not, but tell me, young Jack, am I expected to wait? Am I expected to stand by and watch her let the Empire slip away, all for the sake of a boy she will tire of in a few short years?"

Jack wondered if he should be frightened, more certain than ever that Lorcan hated him. Had gotten him for the Lady, yes, because she asked—or ordered—but hated him nonetheless.

He drew himself up. *He* was the Lady's son now, and

Lorcan was jealous, but Jack would not be bullied. "What will you do when she finds out I'm her last?" he asked. "I haven't told her the doorway's gone, but I could. Whenever I like." A small victory, but an important one nonetheless. Jack leaned back against the seat, pleased with himself.

"Why does everyone want you?" Lorcan hissed. "The Lady loves you far too much. Your fool of a mother, your real mother, weeping like an infant when you disappeared. As if you are special." His fingers curled and straightened again. A deep breath made his chest rise and fall.

Jack blinked. "S-she cried?" In his entire life, he couldn't remember ever seeing her do so.

Lorcan ignored the question. "Very well. This is how it is to be. Tell me what you wish from me to keep the secret of the doorway."

She cried. Is sad I am gone. "It's really destroyed?" Jack asked, and Lorcan nodded. "All right. Tell me why you won't grow old and how you can speak in my head."

Lorcan paled. "So, you have taken my place," he said, almost to himself. "I may indeed have chosen too well. All right, little Jack, I shall tell you, but not today. I have learned much magic from the faeries, and I will teach you everything I know. On the eve of the new year, when the old dies and all is reborn. I will show you then. Precisely at midnight, when magic is strongest. Watch the clock and I will come for you." His words were softly spoken, and he was smiling, but there was something sharp in them as a needle hides in a shirtsleeve, ready to draw blood.

Christmas Eve came with a fresh blanket of snow, and enormous automatons roamed the streets to clear it, leaving dangerously slick cobbles behind.

The palace was everything Jack wanted it to be. A thousand times better than the bits of holly and glass strung up by Mrs. Pond. He ate himself sick on plum puddings and danced with the Lady, Arabella and the other girls spinning around them in pretty gowns.

Best of all was the pile of presents high as a mountain under a tree hung with golden lamps. "From Duke such-and-such," Arabella would say, carrying in another armful that had traveled across the seas.

"Splendid," cried the Lady. "Everyone is so happy. Are you happy, darling Jack?"

"Yes, Mother." He smiled at her.

It was quite impossible to sleep. Cold though it was, Jack crept from his bed to open the window. A flock of faeries darted inside, wings flapping so rapidly they were simply a blur. He released his dragon from its cage and watched as the creatures chased one another around the lights, golden flames ringing off steely bodies. The faeries screeched when the dragon's tiny, snapping jaws came too close to their feet, and then they would gather in a swarm to descend on it, poking and laughing their metal laughs.

The great clock tower chimed every quarter, and Jack measured the hours till dawn. In Londinium, Dr. Snailwater and Beth and Xenocrates would perhaps eat their Christmas dinner together, Beth's oil in a special goblet for the occasion. In London, Mrs. Pond would already be awake, busy at cooking a fat roast goose.

Only in the dark hours did Jack allow himself to wonder whether they missed him, or if they were so used to his absence from the house while he was away at school that things seemed entirely normal. And then he'd think of the Lady, who wanted him with her all the time.

Dawn broke across the city, barely discernible but for a faint lightening of the layer of clouds. It would snow again today; the air was thick with the smell of it.

"Happy Christmas, your lordship," said Arabella, bustling in. "Good gracious, did you sleep?"

"I'm all right."

"Glad to hear it. The Lady's that excited, she'd scarce stand still to be dressed."

Jack did stand still, up until the exact moment Arabella finished lacing his boots. He ran ahead of her, out of his chamber and down the stairs, through the throne room door to fling himself into the Lady's arms. She laughed with delight and spun him around.

"Presents?" he asked.

"Of course! Lorcan, see to breakfast."

"Right away, Lady. Happy Christmas, young Jack."

Jack nodded to him. A kind of uneasy civility had settled between them after their ride in the carriage. Soon, soon he would learn Lorcan's magic, just as Lorcan had offered in the parlor in London.

The pile of packages seemed to have grown overnight. Possibly it had. Wrapped in thin newsprint and fancy silks and everything in between, from the Lady's subjects and her lords and ladies in the colonies. One faded into another as the stack of wrappings grew taller than Jack himself where he sat on the floor.

Arabella passed him the next, a small box neatly wrapped in shimmering emerald paper. Inside, cradled in a nest of tissue, lay an odd device the likes of which Jack had never seen. "From one of the Desert Dukes, I believe," Arabella said to the Lady.

"You see, Lorcan?" the Lady asked. "They would not be sending him these lovely gifts if we had gone to war. Oh, it is so much *nicer* when we can all be friends."

Jack turned the thing over in his hands. It was almost

like a rounders ball, only a little bit not. Stretched at one end, like an egg. Bronze and brass woven together in thick bands. He turned one and it clicked. Curious. Beginning with the top, he spun each, one by one. *Click, click, click.* He turned the last and the whole fell open, revealing a knot of gears within, a small latch on one side.

The room held its breath, waiting to see what the gadget would do next. The Lady grinned with delight.

Jack flicked the latch. The very instant he did, he knew doing so was a mistake. Trapped inside wasn't the glittering, pink bit of soul that had once escaped from the errant foot in Dr. Snailwater's workshop. No, this was a horrid, black, greasy thing, slick, evil, and alive.

It crawled from the egg ball over the hand that held it, burning, stinging.

Good-bye, little Jack. Lorcan's laughter echoed around Jack's head. *Little, broken Jack.*

Jack began to scream, and everything went dark.

The room—his bedchamber—drifted in and out of focus. Once or twice he thought he saw Arabella, Lorcan, an old man whom he did not know, but these might have been dreams. They might have been nightmares, brought on by the awful pain that oozed slowly from his hand and up his arm. A cup was held to his lips, and he swallowed vile, thick liquid that made everything fuzzy like the snow out-side. Arabella's voice was far away and muffled as she told him a story to soothe his screams. Something about a bird, and fire, but he couldn't pay attention. He slept again.

When Jack awoke, he was alone. Something felt very, very wrong, but he didn't know what. Not at first. Blinking, he looked to the window. Daylight, at least what could be called that in the Empire, fell lazily through the glass between half-open curtains. The gift. He'd been opening a present and it had been strange, terrible. It had hurt his hand.

He looked.

And he began to scream anew.

Arabella came. "Shhhh," she whispered, holding a cool cloth to his forehead. "I beg of you, your lordship, do not wake the Lady. Hollering, she's been, all hours of the day and night. She's having the fleets prepared for war."

"No!" Jack tried to sit up, but Arabella held him down.

"Calm yourself, please, Jack."

She had never called him Jack before. It was enough to surprise him into silence.

"Does it hurt?" she asked.

Jack swallowed. "No." Not a proper sort of pain, at any

rate. But when he lifted his arm and saw the empty space, the stump where his hand should be, where it *had* been until he'd opened the gift, a horrible ache spread throughout him.

Water dripped into his eyes. "You can have a new one made," she said with false brightness. "No soul'll wonder where you came from then, hmmm? You'll be just as the rest of us. You're lucky, really. T'was a magical injury. Those heal right quick, faster than the other sort."

A clockwork hand, just like Dr. Snailwater or the footman at the throne room door or countless others Jack had seen. But it meant . . .

"Is she very angry?" Jack asked. Arabella's smile melted.

"Never seen her in such a rage. Smashed up the whole throne room and the Christmas dinner and half the palace besides. Hanged a dozen people, all at once."

"I want to see her." He could comfort her, tell her he didn't mind a new hand.

"Oh, Jack. It was all I could do to convince her that you shouldn't be sent away until you were healed!"

"She doesn't want me anymore?" Jack asked in a whisper, knowing it was true as he said it. He wasn't perfect anymore. Not whole.

"I'm sure she'll change her mind when she's calmed down a wee bit. Let her have some rest, and you need some, too." Arabella dropped the cloth and rose from the bed to cross the room.

In the days that followed, it seemed the Lady was always resting. She was never in the destroyed throne room when he looked, or in the magnificent library. Arabella brought his meals to him on a tray, hurrying off again before he could ask too many questions.

The wound at his wrist started to heal, replaced by a growing, gaping one in his chest. A suspicion that Mother would not change her mind and that Arabella had said that only to silence him. It led him to wait until he was certain Arabella was in the kitchens, fetching his supper. Jack followed the winding corridors, along thick carpets, past wide-eyed, shadowy portraits.

"Let me in," he ordered the footman at the door to the Lady's chambers. Shocked, the man turned the handle before realizing that perhaps he shouldn't, but the space was already enough for a small boy to slip through.

The Lady sat on a stool covered in plum brocade. Her gown was wrinkled, red lips smeared across her cheek, a messy curl hanging like a broken spring down her neck. The room was a mess. A torn curtain dangled limply from its rod.

"M-Mother?"

"I am nobody's mother," she said, quiet and hoarse. "What are you doing here?"

Heat prickled over Jack's skin, burning hottest at his wrist. "I came to see you."

"How nice." Her eyes were cold and frosted over with tears. "You may leave now."

Sickness churned his belly. "But—"

"I said you may go!" she shouted. "I try so very hard for everything to be fun and pretty. Why must people ruin it for me? You were perfect, and now you are not, and you may go! Already Lorcan is finding me another son. A whole son."

For a moment, Jack cradled the truth in his hands. Lorcan would be furious, but Jack supposed that didn't matter now. What more could either of them do to him?

"No," said Jack, standing straight in the face of her fury. "He isn't. Lorcan broke the doorway to keep me here. Ask him yourself; he'll tell you. He did this to me," he finished, raising his arm.

"LIES!" She lifted something from the table, and it smashed in a shower of sharp light against the wall. "He is the most loyal of all my sons. Performed magic you cannot even conceive of to stay with me forever!"

"What magic?" They deserved each other, to live eternally in this fantastic, horrible place with its beautiful clockwork and dying, choking people. But if there was magic Jack didn't know, a sort he hadn't seen, then perhaps, just perhaps, there would be a way to make the doorway again.

"You think I shall tell you? Foolish child. Get out! Get out! Get out! Never show your face in my palace again!"

Little boys do what they're told.

Jack ran.

CHAPTER EIGHTEEN

The Legend

THERE WAS NOTHING JACK WANTED to take with him, or so he thought. No one tried to stop him as he fled through the palace, down the stairs, out the nearest door. Arabella caught up to him just beyond the palace gates, the hem of her dress streaked with mud and slush.

"Take your creature." His dragon was shut up tight in its cage; she gave him the handle. "'Tis freezing," she chattered, wrapping a warm coat around his shoulders. "There's something in the pocket. I'm sorry." And for a moment, she looked it. "I must get back before she starts up again. Keep care of yourself. You have a place to go?"

He hoped so. Jack trusted almost nothing now. "There's

a doctor, in Harleye Street." If that didn't work, he might be able to find his way to Xeno's house, full of faery nectars and wisps of magic.

"I know of this doctor," said Arabella. "On with you, before you catch your death."

Mrs. Pond used to say that. Arabella was gone before Jack looked in his pockets, and so she didn't see the tears that fell to freeze on his cheeks. He'd thought it gone, the compass that was his only tangible memory of London. Of *home*. Where his real mother had cried when he went missing. Of all the things Lorcan had said to him, that was the one thing about which Lorcan had no reason to lie. The compass needle whirled, but the wood was solid, still warm from Arabella's touch in Jack's one hand.

It took a long time to walk to Harleye Street through the snow, and his lungs began to ache from the filthy air. Many times he nearly slipped on grimy ice, too caught up in thoughts to watch his feet. It came back to him in a rush, his house in Mayfair, the wooden soldiers lined up on shelves, his books. Mrs. Pond and his mother and father, who all comforted him when he was sick or hurt.

There *must* be a way back. Simply must be.

Harleye Street was swathed in gray, the tips of the wrought-iron gates frosted like a gruesome cake. No lamps shone from the windows of Dr. Snailwater's, but Jack climbed to the door, put the cage at his feet, and knocked, pain biting at his chilled knuckles.

A minute passed, then another, and another. He might well have to go to Xeno's after all, and his body protested at the idea of the journey. It would be a terrible walk, with his toes numb inside sodden boots, and Arabella hadn't thought to slip any coins in with the compass, if indeed she'd had any to give. The dragon's cage was heavy, especially as he couldn't switch it from hand to hand for relief.

Finally, the door swung open. Dr. Snailwater gazed at him through bloodshot eyes. The once-white hair had lost its fluff and lay on the doctor's head, a filthy, greasy cap.

"Well, well," said the doctor. "The prince returns. Grow tired of the parades, did you?"

Everybody was angry at him, Jack realized miserably. "I'm sorry I ran off," he said. "It was important. I'll explain, I promise."

The doctor huffed. "Don't fancy you turning to an icicle on my stoop," he said.

Oh, it was blessedly warm inside the workshop. The steam was thick enough to cut, and he blinked several times before he could properly see. As soon as he could, he wished to be blind again.

"What . . . what is that?" he asked, his teeth clicking together, though he was no longer quite so cold. Every

surface of the workshop was spread with wires and gears and the strange sort of skin that Jack had only ever seen on one person. On the table nearest him, toes lay scattered like dominoes. The ribbon Beth always wore in her hair was spread precisely in the middle of another.

Dr. Snailwater's voice shook. "That, lad, was a message from Sir Lorcan. Delivered her in a sack, like she was rubbish. Didn't like that we'd taken you in, which beggars the question of why you are here now," he said, holding the cage up to his eyes to peer at the dragon inside.

"Oh, *Beth*," Jack whispered. He moved between the tables, inspecting each broken part. He hadn't realized until now just how much of a comfort it had been on his walk from the palace, the idea that she would be here. After all, she was the first person he'd met in the Empire and the only one he knew who would understand what had just happened to him. "He killed her." Fury raged through him, a fire he wished could burn Lorcan whole.

"Nice to see you understand," said Dr. Snailwater.

"When?" Jack demanded. The doctor pursed his lips in thought.

"Been a few months. Before it got properly cold, as I recall, because I wasn't worried when she was out a whole night. Daft, seeing as cold makes no difference to her, but . . . She came back the next day, cheerful as anything, and went off again. It was the next day that, that—"

"He's horrible," said Jack. So that was why Beth had never come back through the secret passages to visit him. Lorcan had smashed her to bits, just as he'd once said she should be. "And the Lady is . . . I don't think she's quite right in the head. I think she's been alive too long and it's twisted her somehow."

"What happened, lad?"

Jack backed away from the table which held a stretch of leg, a long crack running over the knee. Facing the doctor, he pulled back the sleeve of his coat.

Dr. Snailwater's face lost what slight color it had. "Which of 'em did that?"

"Lorcan." Jack was sure of it. It was too neat, too ordered, a clockwork plot. Lorcan had wanted to go to war, blamed Jack for the Lady's refusal. If he hadn't already despised Jack, that would still have been enough of a reason. What better way to provoke the Lady than to convince her one of the colonies had harmed Jack? And now Lorcan wouldn't have to teach Jack his magic, if he'd ever intended to at all. Lorcan would have known, of course, that the Lady wouldn't bear to look at Jack after . . .

The doctor busied himself clearing one of the tables, turning each piece over in his hands and staring at it for a long time before he set it down to move on to the next. When he had space to work, he fetched boxes and jars, his bag of tools.

"Why haven't you put her back together?" Jack asked.

"I should think," said the doctor, "that since you arrived on my doorstep—for the second time, I might add—that I should be the one to ask the questions. Shall I be expecting another visit from Sir Lorcan?"

"No."

"Right, well, 'spose that's a start. Out with it."

Jack found the stool so often used by Beth while he and Dr. Snailwater had worked on hands, feet, lungs. Before his time at the palace. Before the hangings, which was really where the story began. As the doctor worked, Jack told him about everything but for the voices. Dr. Snailwater didn't seem in a mood to tolerate madness at the moment, particularly from Jack, who thought he couldn't blame him.

"Xeno said . . . Mr. Fink said there might be a way to get home."

The doctor picked up a turnscrew and tightened the joint of a finger. "The only marbles Xeno has left are his eyes."

"But what if there is? I want to go back, Doctor. I didn't before, and I do now."

"Aye, it was plain as crackers you didn't before. As for what that lunatic meant, you'll be asking him yourself. I don't know the whole tale; I've never cared to. Superstition and nonsense."

It must be strange, Jack thought, to have been born here, to have grown up around the faeries and airships and mushrooms with tongues. Perhaps he was more willing to believe whatever Xeno's story was, since *everything* here was so odd to him.

But then, he hadn't heard it yet.

"Can we visit him? I'll wear the goggles if I must, but I don't think it matters overmuch now. They're not looking for me anymore."

Clank, clank, clank. The doctor hammered out a tiny bit of brass. "No need. Truth be told, I thought it was him knocking on the door when you came. He's always pestering me now. Seems to think I'm lonely without . . . with no company. That, and he keeps offering to find me a soul."

"You need one for Beth. That's why you haven't put her together."

A rubber silence stretched loud enough to twang in Jack's ears. "Yes, and no. A whole soul's not the easiest item to procure, even by Xeno's methods, which are best not inspected with more care than necessary. There's no guarantees she'll end up anything like she was, and one like Beth's not so easy to simply replace. Near perfect, she was. My best work. I'll do no better."

Jack understood. The doctor loved Beth as a daughter, more than the Lady ever had, he was sure, and to leave her in bits was possibly more tempting than to see her whole, and different.

"Show me," the doctor barked, pointing to Jack's wrist. Jack raised it aloft.

"Another day, maybe two. Must let it heal properly. I'll have the new one ready by then."

"Thank you," said Jack, aware that this was a kindness he didn't necessarily deserve. But he wanted it, not only to have the use of two hands again.

. . .

Later, much later, when the sky was dark and the air tasted of starlight, Jack crept downstairs, full from supper, warm from the cozy sitting room. The dragon was asleep, contented by a thimbleful of oil. The doctor's hands had shaken to put it inside the cage. He touched a sparkmaker to a lamp, watched it flare to life. The pieces of Beth shone dully in the flame. Her head had broken like the shell of a breakfast egg; it took him a long while to find all the parts.

He would wait for Xeno to come and for his new hand to be fixed to him. And then, if the doctor wouldn't put her back together, Jack would do it himself.

At precisely nine o'clock the following morning, Xeno knocked on the doctor's door. From his stool, Jack heard them speak in low voices on the step before they came inside. Xeno carried a large brandy bottle, stoppered with cork and wax, filled with sky-blue mist.

"I grew tired of your bellyaching, Mephisto. Finest I could get," he told the doctor, grinning with his brass jaw.

"The brandy, or the soul?"

"Both, in fact." Xeno's cracked eye fixed on Jack. "Hullo, Jack. Seems you have a story to tell, but Mephisto's given me the, ah, salient details. You all right?"

"Yes," Jack answered, nodding.

"Shame about the hand, but we can fix that."

"Already started. Up, upstairs with the pair of you. Jack has a question, and if I'm to sit through this madness, I'd just as soon do so with a cup of tea, if it's all the same to everyone."

Dr. Snailwater took longer over the tea than usual, fussing nearly as much as Arabella would with sugar tongs and a plate of biscuits. When he could find no more with which to fidget, he took the last armchair. Jack looked down at the space where his hand should be, used to be, would be again.

"You said there was a legend," he said. "Something that might help me get back through the doorway. But it's broken now, so I reckon what we need is a new one and—"

"Aha," interrupted Xeno, a wide smile spreading across his face as Jack looked up. "You are asking after the story of the Gearwing."

"Long ago, this land was nothing but gods and magic. Some say one came from the other, but that's for another time. The gods hammered at their anvils, forged in white-hot fires. Their creations amused them, and gods love amusement.

"The land changed a bit. People came. They saw what was around them, used it for their own inventions of steam and clockwork, oil and air. The Lady ruled over the Empire, and under her it grew. And, one day, she decided to give the Empire a gift, a kindness for the people she had brought here. A fantastic creature, a symbol of hope and beauty. She used up nearly all her magic building this wonderful thing, but the end result was worth it. Even if it meant that her subjects had to toil twice as hard, construct factories twice as big to do the work she could no longer achieve with magic to keep the Empire safe and prosperous.

"Deep in a cave no sunlight touched, the Gearwing lived in darkness, until the moment came where it made its own light. Aglow with flame and power, it flew out under the sky. Below, anyone fortunate enough to see it caught their breath, said a prayer, and went on with their business— whatever business that might be—happier than before.

"But this," said Xeno, "was not the power of the Gearwing."

"What was?" asked Jack, voice no more than a whisper in the hush that had taken over the room. The story seemed familiar, somehow, but new, too. He closed his eyes, remembering pain and Arabella's voice.

Xeno held a bony finger to his gleaming mouth. "The people loved their faeries, mischievous beasts that they are, the dragons large and small, for they had never known anything else. Griffins with great brass scales and talons were spotted often in the mountains; mechanical unicorns, ever shy, hid their copper horns in the forests.

"But none, none was more loved than the Gearwing. High in the treetops it sang, music unlike any other. Its voice was sweetest in birch, loudest in applewood, and any lucky enough to hear it had their heads filled by beautiful thoughts, as if spoken in their ears.

"This, however, was not the only power of the Gearwing, nor the most important.

"Time is a different thing to different people—long and insufferable to some, a single blink to others. But if it must be measured by one of our many clocks, the Gearwing flew for fifty years before the time came when it made its own darkness. One by one, the metals of it would rust or weather until they no longer gleamed beneath sun but caught the light and held it in dull, scratched places.

"That was not the worst of it, or best, depending on how you looked.

"Soon after, the Gearwing would take itself to seclusion. Caves were its preference, but as the Empire grew, an unused attic or the loft of an abandoned barn would do. There, it let itself crumble, cogs and plates and gears falling, *plink, plink, thunk*. And wherever they fell, they stayed, alive but in parts, like a person who has lost a leg but knows the leg is out there still, and perhaps the leg knows, too.

"And the Gearwing would wait. Beyond its nest, the Empire would seem to grow darker without its light, its song, though how much of that is made up is anyone's guess.

"It never took long. Someone would always find it, be called to it by a sense that perhaps can't be named or described. Perhaps they came upon it while looking high and low for a spool of string, or while scrubbing a home top to bottom in spring. And because they knew, because everyone knew, the finder would count each piece, one, two, three, to ensure all were there. And they would know they had all they needed to put the Gearwing back together.

"A tricky process, to be sure, but worth it in the end. The feet are simplest, for the talons look like nothing else. When one builds a house, it's always best to start from the ground and work up. So, too, with the Gearwing. The legs, the body full of fiddly innards, the tiny, maddening parts that must be assembled into the clockwork heart, *tick*, *tick*. This goes inside the chest before the wings are put on, gear by feather by gear. And the head, the beak, the addition of which was the final thing before it was wound.

"Only then could the Gearwing open its pointed mouth in a musical cry, bittersweet and beautiful, a cry to summon a flame. No one knew from where the flame appeared, but they'd watch as the Gearwing swallowed it and look closely, for the rust would clear from every surface as the soul healed the Gearwing from within. Tarnish disappeared from brass, and an enormous red-gold bird would spread its wings, but not fly away."

Jack couldn't help himself. "Why doesn't it fly away?"

"Because the Gearwing needs us as we need it," Xeno said. "It can't put itself together. And so it grants a miracle to whoever reassembles it."

"What sort of miracle?"

"Anything you could possibly desire." Xeno sipped his tea, surely chilled by now. "Riches beyond imagining. The affection of your beloved. A doorway, perhaps, to another world." This last he said with his glass eyes on Jack, waiting for him to understand. "Only then does it leave in a flight of fire, off to sing in the trees until it is time for it to die again."

"If I could find it, it could send me home."

"Stuff and nonsense," said Dr. Snailwater, speaking for the first time since Xeno's tale began. "I will not have you pinning the lad's hopes on a story best saved for bedtime. There will be another way. We simply have to find it."

The books of faery tales that weighted Jack's shelves in the other London were dead things, crumbling paper and bleeding ink and faded leather. But everything in them had become real here in this one. He thought of the pages of phoenixes, birds of red cunning and golden artifice. They squawked, flew, died, and were reborn from their ashes.

"There's a whole room at the palace full of statues and paintings of golden birds and fire," Jack said. "Beth showed it to me."

"When?" the doctor asked.

Jack was spared having to answer by Xeno, who leaned forward. "How big were these statues, boy?"

"Er." He thought back. "None much bigger than I am, I'd say."

Xeno's shoulders slumped. "Well, it's not there. The legend has always maintained the creature is very large. Pity. It'd be clever, hiding it among a pile of imitations. Hm."

"It can't just've disappeared," said Jack.

"You would think not," Xeno agreed. "But it has, shall we say, been dark here for a very long time. There's none that's alive who remembers it, save perhaps the Lady and Sir Lorcan. Given the state of things, I don't imagine they'd be much inclined to help."

No, they would not. But excitement filled Jack regardless. It was out there somewhere, waiting. He knew it now, yet more when he turned his head to see the doctor's odd crystal ball, glinting in the morning light.

The crystal ball might only show the past, but it did show the truth. "You believe in that," Jack said, pointing.

"I can *see* that, plain as the nose on my face. No one has ever come up with more than a tall tale of this bird."

It was no longer a time for secrets.

"I saw the Gearwing," Jack said. "In the ball. First there was Lorcan, following me through the train station. But after, it went all misty and then a great bird flew from it, and I thought the ball had smashed, only it hadn't, not really."

Carefully, very slowly, Xeno put down his teacup. "When was this?"

"After I met Beth and she brought me here. That first night."

"Aha, yes, when you were touching things that didn't belong to you," said Dr. Snailwater, but there was no meanness in it. "Something gave you a shock that night, to be certain, but to think it was this myth is lunacy. Sheer lunacy! Even if I were to allow for the possibility, as men of my ilk must be open to different theories, it could be anywhere. In a cave that will never be found, or scattered in a thousand bits at the bottom of the Thames!"

"That much is true." Xeno stood, stretching his legs. "We shall have to think, and however much of a fool you think me, Mephisto, I don't say we should stop looking for a different answer. One way or another, Jack must go home."

They fell to talk of the soul Xeno had brought and of the hand Dr. Snailwater was crafting for Jack, but Jack himself was silent, concentrating. Something nagged at the edges of his mind. A thought, darting away on faery wings each time he got too close. The doctor and Xeno left him, footsteps thumping their way down to the workshop, but as the sky outside grew thick with snow and the room dimmed to night black in the middle of the day, still, it wouldn't come.

CHAPTER NINETEEN

Lorcan, Banished

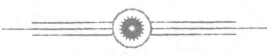

WHEN LORCAN WAS SUMMONED to the Lady, he went with a spring in his step. The boy was gone, injured beyond healing. Lorcan was once again the Lady's only son.

"Lady," he said, entering her rooms. Everything was broken or torn, but her sadness would pass. It was a good thing for her to be reminded just how breakable people were, that it didn't do to place all one's affection in them.

"Lorcan, dearest." Warmth flushed through him as she rose from her stool. "You have readied the fleets? The Desert Duke will be punished?"

"As you wished, Lady, of course."

"Curious, that one should scheme to harm Jack after I'd

already decided on peace. That the colonies were welcome to rule themselves with no interference from us. Don't you find that curious?" She gazed impassively at him, but the scent of danger filled the room. Surely the boy hadn't . . .

"He said a strange thing before I sent him away. He said it was you." The Lady stepped closer. "That cannot be true, can it? You wouldn't wish unhappiness on me, would you, Lorcan?"

No, no. He had only ever acted to bring her joy. Except this time. This last time. "Lady, I can—"

"I should kill you where you stand!" she hissed. "But you have stolen even that satisfaction from me, with your wicked magic. If you hadn't broken the thing already, I *would break you.*" Her eyes shone. "You will go, Lorcan. Far away. I wish never to set eyes on you again, and you will live forever alone."

When Lorcan was banished, he retreated to the farthest-flung corner of the island to wait. He'd had no choice but to hurt the boy. The Lady would come to understand soon enough. He would simply not be turned into a useless lump by a mere stripling of a boy.

It was his own failing; he knew that now. The Lady was all that was generous and good, and Lorcan, magic notwithstanding, was simply a man.

She would forgive him for breaking the doorway; she always pardoned him for his crimes in the end. Eternity was a terribly long time for anger to fester. She would grow lonely, and she would love him again. Welcome him home as the good son he'd always been. He had told the truth of what he'd done to the boy, and the doorway, when she asked, as a good son did.

Briefly, he'd wondered whether it might not be the best plan simply to kill the boy for telling the Lady his secret, but Lorcan was far too experienced in war tactics to make such an amateur error.

It was best to leave one's enemies alive, wounded, in fear. Naturally, the boy had fled to that fool doctor, just as Lorcan had expected, but what could they do? Little Jack would have seen the oddity, smashed to pieces, and surely now was cowering, certain of Lorcan's power, the lengths to which he would go if he must.

No, Lorcan's biggest regret was that there had been no time to check his particular hiding places in the city before he left. But they were safe, safer than ever. This, he could feel. He had to thank London for that: their architects and city planners giving him such convenient spots to protect his treasures. Before, he'd moved them from one place to another, never keeping them anywhere too long. Permanence was a relief; he need not worry about them now. They need not even be guarded. Better that they weren't, in fact, as someone might ask why.

"Trinket," he said very quietly. Ridiculous name, truly, but it had not been his choice, and the creature would answer to nothing else.

The imp came running, slipping, tumbling over the deck of the ship. Moored in the lee of a mountain, sheltered from the battering wind and snow. The imp shivered and Lorcan smiled. He was never cold.

"News, Trinket?"

"N-none, sir." There had been no messengers, no faeries with notes clutched in needle-fingers. London could have burned to the ground and he would not know.

Except that he would.

Oh, she would see that he had done it all for her. She had accused him of being jealous, of all things! Jealous of a silly child. But she was clever, the Lady, and when the boy was forgotten, the hurts healed, he would take the Empire to war, expand it to the very edges of the earth for her to rule.

For that is what a good son did.

CHAPTER TWENTY
Beth, Whole Again

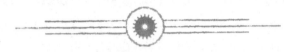

J ACK FLEXED HIS NEW HAND, awed by its intricacy. A thick, copper sleeve, lined with silk, stretched halfway up to his elbow.

Thanks didn't seem to be quite enough, but Dr. Snailwater appeared not to want them. He simply grunted and turned away to look, yet again, at the pieces of Beth on his workbenches.

The hand felt slightly stiff, unused, which of course it was, but it did what he asked of it. After a fashion. Experimentally, he pinched a gear between two fingers. It held for an instant, clattered to the floor.

"You're not thinking, lad. The idea of the hand is still there. Tell it what you want."

Face scrunched, Jack concentrated. The brass rods began to move, gears at the knuckles to spin. This time, he gripped the gear for several seconds between his fingertips.

He practiced and practiced and practiced some more, staying awake long after the doctor retired for the night. Curled on his pallet of blankets, he practiced. He didn't much want to thank Lorcan, but it was a great deal more interesting than a normal hand. Soon, the doctor gave him simple puzzles, small gadgets to assemble or fix. All the while, Beth lay scattered on the tables below.

He certainly didn't want to thank Lorcan for anything.

"You must do it, Mephisto, or decide not to," said Xeno, come to admire Jack's hand. "Don't leave her cluttering up the place."

The soul in the brandy bottle swirled, its light pulsing stronger as Xeno came near.

"Why does it do that?" Jack asked, pointing with one of his new fingers.

"Well, see, I captured it, so it thinks it belongs to me. But I've already got a soul, tarnished though it may be, so they're having a little argument among themselves over which should boss me about. Best I don't get involved."

"But it'll be Beth's, when she's put back together," said Jack.

"Indeed it will. Mephisto, please. The sensation is really rather unpleasant."

"We should be looking for a way to get him back home," said the doctor, gesturing to Jack with his teacup.

"Please," said Jack. "I want to help." He'd already been away from London so long, his parents must think him dead by now. Or worse. Another short time made no difference. It felt wrong to leave Beth like this, with no chance to say good-bye, even if they knew of a way to re-create the doorway, which they did not. No way other than the Gearwing, hidden who-knew-where so that it might as well not be real at all.

"All right," said the doctor, taking a deep breath. "All right."

They got to work. Xeno, being mostly concerned with souls and faery magic, stood out of the way and watched, cracked eye wobbling to and fro. Dr. Snailwater cleared a place for his tools, lining them neatly up on a strip of cloth.

The first day, they sorted through the pieces, unscrewing and separating one from the next, which made Jack think of Xeno's story about the Gearwing and how all the parts must be counted. Now and again the doctor realized one was missing, or too damaged from the fall to be used. Metals were heated, shaped on lathes, cooled in buckets of water that hissed angrily.

It was a painstaking task, and Jack fell onto his blankets after supper, relieved to close eyes still stinging from the steam. Hours passed in a single blink; the parlor was filled with morning. Over a hasty breakfast, Jack wondered how long it had taken Dr. Snailwater to build Beth the first time. The twelve others who had come before her, too, now gone forever.

But he did not ask.

Long copper pipes rolled over the tabletops, and thin ones the width of a pin.

The doctor gave Jack a box. "You should remember the foot."

Jack did. The challenge was only in getting his hand to cooperate, but after a while he found that his new fingers could be quick and clever if he let them. From the feet, he moved to her hands, surprised by how like his new one they were, leastways beneath the strange skin that would cover her later. Hunched over gears and hinges for days on end, neck aching, the mysterious thought continued to hide from him. It was as if his mind were a palace, with too many rooms behind closed doors, too many wardrobes into which small thoughts could escape.

There was something. *Something*.

"Pass me the measure; there's a lad," said the doctor.

Jack gasped.

Beth.

Not whole again, not nearly, but he could see the shape

of what she'd be. Unborn, still growing, a promise of a girl with a ribbon in her hair. Bones and joints, thin tubes to run slick with her cups of oil. Innards of cogs and gears, ready to move when her key was finally turned.

Muttering something about an improved sense of time, the doctor measured the knot of workings that would become her brain, then straightened up. From his pockets came a handful of coins to clatter on the table.

"I'll be doing the rest," he said. "I daresay you can go for a walk now to fetch some supper, seeing as no one's looking for you. Wrap up warm, mind, and don't get lost."

Jack scowled. He'd helped, hadn't he? And now Dr. Snailwater wanted to do all the good bits himself. He left the house bundled and sulky, kicking at the snow with his boots. Too late, it struck him that the doctor wanted to finish Beth alone, in order to have the last hours in which she was the same in his memory as she'd always been.

Jack wandered with no particular place in mind. It was too cold for thinking of particular places, and he didn't know where he was headed until the familiar-but-not streets of Mayfaer stretched before him. A curious warmth spread inside. He hadn't meant to look for it and wasn't even certain he could have found his way if asked to. In the other London, surely he would've been lost before now, but his time here had taught him a great many things.

The factory stretched an entire block, icicles hanging from the eaves but otherwise the same as when he'd first seen it with Beth. He remembered the half terror, half excitement he'd felt then at the sudden, certain proof that he was a long way from home.

With his metal fingertips, chilled to the touch though they didn't feel it, Jack reached for the filthy bricks. A sheen of grime came away on his hand.

On the other side of a doorway, Mother and Father were there. Drinking tea, perhaps, or sat down to dinner.

Weeping, again, at the loss of their son. Jack did not like to hope for this, and yet . . .

"Oy!"

Jack spun, nearly slipped on the ice. A big, burly man stood ten feet away, pale gray as everything around them but for mean slashes of pink high on pockmarked cheeks. "H-hello," he said.

"Nothing 'ere for stealing," said the man.

Jack shook his head. "No, no sir, I was only—" But the man wouldn't believe him if Jack explained, and so he closed his mouth.

The man took a step toward him. "You look mightily familiar, boy. Have I seen you snooping around before?"

He pursed his lips and snapped his fingers. "Yeah, I've seen you. All up on your airship with the Lady. Right pleased, the missus was, that the Lady finally had 'erself a son, even without a husband about the place. Best not to talk about that, eh?" The man laughed. The sound was as sticky as the dirty snow.

"I'm not . . . not him," Jack said fiercely. It wasn't quite an untruth. The boy who'd lived at the palace felt like an old Jack, a different Jack, as a snake that sheds its skin. A brief, sparkling time during which it had been far too easy to forget things he ought've remembered.

He looked at the factory wall again.

"Hmph. You might be right. I'm sure that one had both his hands. Shame. Would've been a story to tell. Off with you, then, if you're not royalty I should invite to tea." The man sauntered off, hobnailed boots crunching.

"I'm coming back, Mother," Jack whispered to the wall. "I'm sorry."

When Jack arrived back at Harleye Street, laden with a pie, the doctor wasn't alone. Xeno had arrived, and the air was thick with a fug of expectation. If Jack hadn't known better, he would have said Beth was sleeping, in the way she slept, but something about the skin was too dull, flat. Crude lines of red stitches seamed her limbs not covered by her dress and slashed across her forehead.

He put the pie down none too gently. "She won't always look like that, will she?"

Xeno winked. The crack in the glass made it extremely disconcerting. "Watch."

Together, the doctor and Xeno hoisted Beth to sitting, bending her legs to hang from the edge of the table.

"Allow me," Xeno said as Dr. Snailwater reached for her key, but the doctor shook his head. Slowly, he wound her up, each turn loud in the room, over the machines and the hammering of Jack's heart.

At the final click, Beth's eyes opened. Jack moved closer, drawn in by their odd blankness. She looked from one to the next with no sign of recognition. His stomach sank. Dr. Snailwater was right; she wouldn't be the same.

"The bottle," said the doctor, prizing open her mouth with a gentle thumb on her chin. Xeno reached over with a long arm. Inside the glass, the soul pulsed vibrant blue as his hand wrapped around the neck. "Drink up, Beth. There's a good girl."

Obediently, she drank, the mist sucked from the bottle in great gulps.

Jack stepped closer still, disbelieving. The stitches faded, then disappeared completely, healed from within. Her skin began to brighten, her eyes to spark with life. She drank the very last drop and pushed the bottle away.

"A healthy soul, a healthy body," whispered Xeno to Jack. "One cures the other."

Jack only half listened, far too fascinated all over again by Beth.

"Hello," she said dully. The hairs at Jack's neck tingled. It *sounded* like Beth, but *not* like her, too. She'd always been so cheerful before. "Who are all of you?"

The doctor turned away; Jack thought he saw tears. Xeno put his hand on the doctor's shoulder. "The soul has to heal her insides, too. Give it time, Mephisto. Give it time."

Time, however, was not a friendly thing for a while. Two days and nights passed. Dr. Snailwater wandered the house, muttering to himself that he'd known it would happen. That he never should have listened, or been persuaded to reassemble her.

He barely spoke to Jack, or to Xeno. The second time Beth's key wound down, he forbade anyone to wind it up again. She remembered none of them, and had scarce said a word after those first few.

"What do we do?" Jack asked Xeno, who did not answer straightaway. Instead, his glass eyes swiveled around the workshop, not looking at anything in particular. Upstairs, Beth, who wasn't really Beth, sat unseeing in her chair. The doctor had shut himself away in his rooms.

"We wait," said Xeno after a while. "I've seen this before, once or twice."

"Why does it happen?"

"The brain and the soul must work together," Xeno answered. "Beth's brain is all the same parts as before, but the soul is new. Just like your hand, you know, but a bit the other way around. The essence and the solid, one is near useless without the other. You saw her skin—the soul will heal her, remind her brain of who she is, but she was badly broken. That won't always fix in an eyeblink."

Footsteps thudded on the stairs. Jack and Xeno both looked toward them, watching Dr. Snailwater descend with Beth in his arms, a determined look on his face.

"Enough of this nonsense," said the doctor angrily. "I won't have her taking up space." He set Beth, still as marble, sitting on the edge of a table. "There's good parts in here. I can use them for something else. Perfect measurements. Xeno, get ready to take the soul, if you want it. Worthless thing, if you ask me."

"Mephisto—"

"No!" Jack shouted, running to stand beside Beth. "You can't just take her apart again. You *can't*."

Dr. Snailwater glared at him. "I think you'll find I can do exactly that, lad. And you, you've been nothing but trouble since you got here. Throwing everything into chaos, running away, coming back like ye never left, getting Beth all smashed up. Off with you, if you don't want to see it."

"She was my first friend here," Jack whispered. "I'm sorry, for all of it. I want to go home. Please don't break her again. Don't kill her."

"Mephisto," Xeno began once more. "Over here." He dragged the doctor to the far corner of the workshop; Jack heard them arguing in whispers.

Neither one was looking at him. Perhaps if her eyes were open, if she was moving, the doctor wouldn't be able to do it. Slowly, so as not to attract attention, Jack began to turn Beth's key. When it stopped, her eyelids fluttered and clicked.

"Hello, Jack! You're back! And still ugly, but not so pink! And you have a new hand! Gosh, I feel just like myself again," she said, spying Xeno and the doctor, "and everyone's here. Are we having a party?"

It took some time for a relieved Dr. Snailwater to explain that there had been an . . . accident, but he and Xeno and Jack had put her back together. Beth's head tilted, the way it always had when she was thinking, carefully, of the kind thing to do. "Thank you," she said finally, as the doctor dabbed at his eyes with a rag.

"You're most welcome, dear."

There *was* a festive atmosphere to the place, through supper and tea after, with a fresh bottle of brandy for Xeno and Dr. Snailwater. Beth released the dragon from its cage and it flew lazily around the ceiling, frightening the passengers on the miniature train.

They were something of a family, Jack thought, Beth and the doctor and Xeno, bound together by strangeness thick as any blood. He was very lucky to have found them; where he would be now if he hadn't . . . Jack squirmed to think of it.

But blood mattered too. And perhaps no family was perfect. His was in London, waiting for him to come home. A secret excitement bubbled in Jack at all the things he could tell his father about metals and steam and clockwork. Foster & Sons had been a grand company for many years, and with what Jack had learned in the Empire, he could make it greater still.

If he could only get back.

Xeno took his leave, having to get over the great, frozen Thames to his bed, and soon after, the doctor retired for the night, whistling as he went. Beth, who had been wound much later in the day than usual, sat in her armchair, a book in her lap and her eyes on Jack.

"I was awake, you know," she said. "When they

came for me. I only pretended I wasn't."

Jack thought he might lose his supper. "Did it hurt?"

"No. It was a bit like flying must be, and after that I don't remember anything. Lorcan was in an odd room, filled with odd things. I think he must have been doing magic. The bad sort."

"*He* is horrible," Jack said, sitting on his blankets. And it all came spilling out, the reason for the hangings, and Lorcan, and yes, even the voice he'd heard in his head. The thought he'd been trying to capture for days came close and ran away again, giggling like a faery. He told Beth of his time with the Lady, the cakes and hide-and-seek, steering the airships over the island. Of Christmas Day, the egg in the box, waking in his bed to find his hand was gone. Of the Lady's anger and wanting to go home.

Finally, he told her of Xeno's story, the Gearwing, though this turned out to be quite unnecessary, as she'd heard it before.

"I think it must be real, don't you?" she asked.

"I think," said Jack, sleep beginning to tickle at him, "that it is easy to believe in anything here." His eyes closed, the pillow musty under his head. He could picture it, clear as he'd seen in the crystal ball. Big, nearly, as a dragon, flame-colored, fierce. Swooping, swooping . . .

He did not dream, so he didn't know what woke him

late into the night. Beth, possibly, but no. The book rested open, unseen, on her lap, her key wound fully down. For a time he lay there, comforted by darkness, but it would be light again soon. Another day during which he was in the Empire, cold and clogged with soot. Days would add up to months, years, and he might die here, veins choked with black, none of his family any the wiser about what had become of him.

He couldn't bear it. A deep, terrible sadness washed over him. This place was full of clockwork, ticking away, but not a single one could rewind the time to a few minutes before twelve on a drizzly day spent shopping with Mrs. Pond. He doubted there were any men in the whole Empire cleverer than the doctor and Xeno, and their only answer was a story. True or not, it didn't matter.

Suddenly very much awake, Jack straightened, sat up. He was Jack Foster, which meant very little here but quite a lot in London. Lords and ladies came to supper in his fine house; he would run Foster & Sons one day. This mad, strange, fantastic place would not trap him.

Pushing himself up, Jack looked across the room. It was an unusually clear night, and a rare strip of moonlight shone through the window, turning the crystal ball to a tiny, glowing moon itself. Jack rose from his blankets and crossed the room, past Beth, perfectly motionless. His metal fingertips clinked against the glass as he lifted it to his eyes, right in the path of the moonbeam. "Show me," he whispered, entirely unsure what he hoped to see. Within, the mist swirled slightly.

All was quiet and still. Even the dust was resting, coddled in nooks and crannies. Over and over he commanded the crystal ball, but stubbornly, it showed him nothing.

Jack closed his eyes. Music began to play, far beyond Harleye Street.

He opened them again. It wasn't music, but the beginning of the chimes to mark the hour. Not just any hour, but midnight.

Precisely at midnight, when magic is strongest, Lorcan had said in the carriage. *Watch the clock.* The clock above where the magical doorway had been.

The ball fell from his hands and to the floor with such a thump he was lucky it didn't truly break this time. It rolled beneath an armchair, all but forgotten as Jack ran from the parlor to wake the doctor.

"Dr. Snailwater, please, wake up." Jack grasped his shoulder and shook him, far too excited to think of how rude he was, standing in the doctor's bedchamber at a silly hour. "Please."

The doctor snuffled and blinked, his nightcap askew on his fluffy hair.

"It's real," Jack said urgently as the doctor sat up.

"Hmph?"

"The Gearwing. It *is* real, and I know where it's hidden."

CHAPTER TWENTY-ONE

The Ticking Clock

FOR THE SECOND TIME, JACK left Dr. Snailwater's in the darkness, but now he was not alone. Beth, freshly wound by Jack's shaking fingers, followed with the doctor, keeping up as best they could as Jack ran through the snow. He did not stop to watch the faeries in the lamplight, or to answer the questions that rang out behind him.

They would see. It all made so much more sense if he showed them. An imp had been summoned, bribed with oil to dash all the way to the East End on nimble feet. The night lay overhead, a shroud of cold. Jack looked up, a handful of bright points in the sky visible through a thin layer of the clouds that gave the Empire its name.

"Madness," muttered Dr. Snailwater. Jack ignored him, for it wasn't madness. Soon they would understand.

He could smell the river, brackish and ice and starlight, none of the stink of summer. The thing was close; he could feel it. This must be how Lorcan felt. Fear sliced through Jack; Lorcan might be close, too.

But Jack's steps faltered only a little.

A figure waited for them at the mouth of the bridge, jaw shining.

"Do tell me why I had cold water poured on my head in the dead of night, Mephisto," said Xeno, stamping the snow from his boots. "Some of us enjoy our sleep."

The doctor leaned upon the railing over the river, breath coming in alarming gasps. Perhaps they should have hailed a carriage, or taken one of the trains that rumbled below. But Jack's regret was forgotten as he turned to Xeno.

"I know where the Gearwing is," Jack said. Immediately, Xeno appeared to have been awake for hours.

"Dragged . . . halfway across . . . dead of night," gasped the doctor. "For this . . . nonsense."

"It's *not* nonsense," Jack insisted, turning slowly. He tilted his head to the unusually clear sky, pointing up. "It's the clock. I didn't think of it when you first told the story, but you have to believe me. I've seen it. Not just in the crystal ball. I've *seen* it."

He was going to go home. Happiness bubbled through him, fizzy as bright, sunny sherbet lemons. "A clock is just parts. All little parts, big ones. What matters is how they're put together."

They had to see for themselves. Without a word, Jack took off for the base of the tower. There were no guards this time, just the plain wooden door with a round brass handle.

And a lock. Jack slumped. Of course there would be, and he'd been daft not to think of it.

Without a word, Xeno slipped around him, pulling something needle thin and glinting from a tattered pocket. The *click* seemed dreadfully, shockingly loud; Jack jumped and turned to look past Beth and the doctor. No one else was anywhere in sight, all sensibly in their homes, huddled up for warmth.

"After you," said Xeno grandly, ushering Jack inside. It was just as he remembered, the dark room and the door leading to the stairs. Faint light came in through the windows, which made climbing as much a matter of feeling as seeing. Jack heard Dr. Snailwater's strained breath, Beth's clickety knees, Xeno's footsteps right behind him.

Ears straining, he listened for sounds overhead, but none came. None but rhythmic, ticking movement.

His head ached with remembering how many doors

he'd passed before he came to the enormous clock on that day so many months before. Higher and higher they went, until they could feel the frigid air blowing down from the belfry directly overhead, open to the skies.

"In here," Jack said, mouth dry. The room was pitch-black, scented with grease. Of course Lorcan would keep it running, a smooth, oiled trap, the Gearwing a bird in a cage fashioned of itself.

"I can't see a blind thing," said Beth. There was a tapping sound as someone—Xeno or the doctor, Jack couldn't guess—felt along the wall and the snap of a sparkmaker held to a lamp. The flame burst to life, casting golden shadows across the floor, bouncing off the huge clockwork mechanism, half as big as the room.

"Oh," Beth breathed. "Oh."

It was all there, or nearly so, and Jack had the answer for the other parts, knowing the question would come. A clock, yes, but even now, looking at it through the eyes of all he'd learned in the Empire, he could see that cog as part of a leg, that gear the center of a wing.

Xeno gazed at it, aglow as a man possessed. "The whole time," he whispered. "Right here under our noses. Or above them, really."

"It used to break," said Jack to himself. "When I first came, someone told me it was broken, but it was only broken here, not on the other side of the door. It broke again just before the hangings began. I think he went back to London then. He didn't like to leave it whole and working when he was somewhere he couldn't see it, but he has to have it running when he's here because that's part of the magic of it. When he was in my house he had bits of it in his pocket. I know because he dropped them and I picked one up."

What a very long time ago that had been.

There was more. Finally, Jack let go of his last secrets, explaining how, in London, Lorcan had waited for the clock to chime twelve so that he could open the doorway. The voice, the horrible voice, *Lorcan's* voice, the description of which made Dr. Snailwater whiten beneath his reddened, sweaty face. The voice that was the thought which had nagged at Jack like an itch, because this was one of the powers of the Gearwing and he hadn't truly grasped it straightaway. Most of all, the curious behavior of the soul in the brandy bottle, how it had argued with Xeno's, because he'd caught it and so, for a time, had two souls instead of the more normal one.

"Lorcan's *using* it somehow," said Jack, aware that he probably sounded quite mad now. "It's how he can talk inside my head—anyone's, probably, if he wants to. Because the Gearwing can do that, you said. And it's why he's never died. He's never let this fall apart, like it's s'posed to, so it stays alive when it shouldn't, like him. Only it's a bit dead, at the same time, too, because it's not itself now."

Magic you cannot conceive of.

The Lady knew. Perhaps she had been the one to tell Lorcan of the Gearwing, or discovered his secret only after he'd done this awful thing. But he'd told her it was destroyed, which wasn't quite true.

"He's an evil, murdering—" Xeno paused, then said something that would've earned him a right hiding from Mrs. Pond, no matter how old he was. He reached out to lay a hand on one of the gears. "Ah, you poor creature."

All together, the four inspected the workings, crouched down and leaning over as it ticked slowly on. It was beautiful like this, as a clock, Jack thought. Terribly, tragically beautiful and wrong. Like turning his lovely little dragon into a teakettle, but so very much worse.

Beth wandered from the room, up a short flight of stairs. The clock gave a loud, shuddering *thunk,* and Jack followed her just in time to see the hammer strike the grandest bell he had ever seen. Cast iron, big enough for a man to stand in. He clapped his hands over his ears, the chime echoing through his brain.

Once. Twice. A third time. The hammer stopped.

"That," said Beth, "was extremely loud."

Jack couldn't answer. His teeth were still wobbling. Above the largest bell were four smaller ones, still nearly bigger than Jack, to ring the quarters. All hung from the roof, but wind blew in from the open sides of the belfry. Jack crept to the edge, the city spread below. Plumes of steam shot up here and there; lamplight shone. An automaton, small as a beetle from this great height, cleared a street of snow. On the other side, the river slugged along, chunks of ice brushing together only to drift apart again.

The doctor and Xeno had joined them to marvel at the bell, but the doctor's face was screwed up in thought.

"Hold up," he said. "Where's the feathers?"

Triumph flashed through Jack. "The hands, on the faces, and the bits that mark the minutes. You can't see them half the time anyhow; everything's usually covered in clouds. Nobody noticed." And why would they? Choking, sooty disease got them all too soon. Barely anyone would remember the clock's construction. To most, it was the same as it had always been.

"All right," said Dr. Snailwater. "I'm a man of evidence; it may be true, as you say, but we can't go taking apart the thing just because we think we could build a daft great bird from it for lack of a better way to spend the afternoon, even if it will send you home. Which remains to be seen, regardless. We certainly can't carry it down piece by piece."

No, that'd take ages. Someone would notice before they were halfway done. But Jack had thought of this already, and he had a plan. He simply needed Arabella's help.

Waiting for Arabella to come, Jack imagined he could feel every tick of the clock. Every second, trapped in a place, a shape, it shouldn't be. And with each minute, his anger grew at all the horrible things Lorcan had done. The hangings, and keeping Jack in the Empire, and his hand, and the Gearwing, and so much more besides. Jack had taken to carrying a pair of the doctor's binoculars around his neck everywhere he went, slipping fiendlike through the streets until he could catch a glimpse of the tower.

The clouds had moved in again, heavy and dark. Often, the most he could see was the very bottom edge of the clock face turned to him.

Three days passed before Arabella was able to slip from the Lady's clutches for an hour. She arrived panting for breath, clutching her side, as if she'd run the whole distance from the palace. A pretty scarf covered her hair and half her face when the doctor answered the knock.

"'Lo, Arabella," said Beth, to Jack's surprise. He'd quite forgotten Beth's time with the Lady, what with everything else.

Arabella removed her scarf so that they could see her nervous smile. "Hello, Beth, m'duck. I've not got long; she's expecting me back. Thinks I've only run to find fresh roses. If someone might tell me why a faery walloped my head until I read this"—she held up a tiny scrap of paper— "I'd much appreciate it." Her eyes went to Jack's new hand and softened slightly.

"I'm sorry," said Jack. He *had* asked Xeno to make sure the faery was a persistent sort. "We—that is, I—need help, and I thought perhaps you would."

"I daresay that depends what it is."

He told her.

Her eyes widened. "You cannot just steal one, your lo— Jack! You'll have half the fleet after you!"

"We need it," he insisted.

"Might I ask what for?"

"I think it best that you don't know," said the doctor from behind Jack. "So that if anyone asks, you can say you had no earthly idea of it."

Arabella gave the doctor a long look. "This is about getting 'im home, I suspect." Jack goggled at her, and she smiled again. "It's a funny thing," she said, "but when you don't ask too many questions, people tend to forget you's in the room. Gives a person lots of time to hear all the answers."

All his stay at the palace, Jack had liked Arabella, but now he looked at her with a new kind of respect. She was very nice, really, and clever when she wanted to be.

"I've gone around the twist," she said to herself. "But all right. I'll do as I can. No promises, mind. Things are all a bit funny at the moment."

Jack swallowed. "How is she?" It made him sad to think the Lady was still upset, no matter how unkind she'd been to him in the end. She was only old, and lonely, and Lorcan had stolen the beautiful gift she had given her Empire. And Mother—his *real* mother—had only been busy, unsure what to do with him when he was home from the school Father insisted he attend. She didn't know him at all, but he didn't know her much, either.

Arabella *must* help him.

"Not well," answered Arabella sadly. "Spends her days shut up in her rooms; only lets me and a few of the other girls in to tidy and bring her supper and whatnot. Oh, it's been terrible, and she had such a row with Lorcan. She banished him, if you can believe. He ran off with his tail between his legs, and she won't tell anyone why. They say he's up in the mountains, and good riddance, too." She clapped her hand to her mouth.

Jack knew why, but he held his tongue and tried to appear surprised. Better, as the doctor said, that she not know more than she must. But a small part of the Lady must have believed what Jack had told her about Lorcan, enough to confront him. And Lorcan hadn't been able to lie to her.

"I liked it at the palace," said Beth, after Arabella had spied one of the doctor's small clocks and run out with a yelp. "Sad that the Lady's all alone now."

Dr. Snailwater patted her on the head, as he did so often when Beth showed a kindness. There was nothing to do now but wait for Arabella to send word. The doctor tried to keep Jack amused by giving him bits and pieces to do in the workshop, but Jack's thoughts were ever on the clock that wasn't. Was it in pain? Did it know, in the way his hand knew what it should be, or was it more like Beth, who felt nothing after Lorcan broke her to bits?

The moon was over the thick clouds when a faery tapped on the window, scrap of paper in hand. Arabella wished them luck. The doctor gave the faery an egg cup of oil and shooed it on its way, for little ears were still capable of listening, and it'd be just like a faery to cause trouble.

Of course, their plans depended on that; it just had to be *their* sort of trouble.

Xeno arrived, arms full of jewel-bright nectars, oils flavored with flowers and spice, which clung to the glass inside the bottles. Quite the sight they made, a short time later, pushing their way through the thick steam on the train platform and jostling into a compartment. A sack of tools hung from the doctor's shoulder, weighing it down several inches below the other. Beth smiled at everyone she saw; some smiled absently back, others skulked away.

Jack fiddled impatiently with the knobs on his binoculars.

A short way outside Londinium, the train rose above the ground, chugging through fields frosted black with the last of the snow. It lay in shapeless lumps, large coals that burned with ice, not fire. Even these disappeared the farther south they ventured, so everything—the land, the sky above—was dark gray with night.

They were the only ones to alight at the station listed in Arabella's note, which was nowhere near a town or a factory, nor anything a person might want to visit. The conductor gave them a curious look through the open window of his carriage, but if an oddly assembled bunch wanted to traipse around the countryside in the dead of night, it was no concern of his.

It wasn't far to walk, which was perhaps just as well. The tools clanked inside the sack as Dr. Snailwater huffed and puffed, and Jack took an armful of bottles from Xeno after the second time of catching one just before it fell to the

ground. Over a hill, through a dark thicket of trees run with nightly creatures whose chatter hinted of iron and steel.

The airships spread out against the horizon, a half dozen of them in a row neat as a line of buttons, lamps scattered on their decks. Billow-sailed, hulls gleaming, they hovered twenty feet above the fields, ready to rise at the first call.

"That one," said Jack quietly, pointing to the very end. It was only sense not to choose one in the middle.

"Your shout, Xeno," said the doctor.

The bottles clinked. Xeno whistled a sweet, pretty tune, all the richer for the warm brass of his jaw, and the sky turned silver.

Faeries, thousands upon thousands of them, descended on the four, a roaring hailstorm of fluttering, wicked metal wings. Xeno waved a bottle of nectar at the one in front of his face and gave instructions, which passed from faery to faery in tinny, cackling whispers. As quickly as they had come, they were gone, swooping off in a dense cloud toward the ship. Beth clapped her hands. All four held their breath.

"Oy!"

"Attack!"

"Pointy wee blighters! Argh!"

The shouts rang out on the deck. Jack lifted the binoculars to his eyes, and it was difficult not to laugh at the utter mayhem. Faeries ripped plumes from helmets; soldiers found their pistols dangled just out of reach. A whole clutch of the creatures swarmed the captain, poking and pulling at him until he abandoned the wheel.

"Save yourselves!" he bellowed. "That's an order, chaps!"

The other ships, roused by the noise, ran to their cannons and raised their guns. Laughter filled the air as the faeries spread out, and soon not a single ship was spared.

From the belly of the first, the airship Jack wanted, the ramp opened. He remembered ascending one just like it with the Lady and Lorcan. Its edge was still several feet from the ground when the first men tumbled down, two of them landing with horrid, squishy thumps, never to rise again.

Jack tried to shut that from his mind.

The plan was working. Soldiers ran past in a line, paying no mind at all to Jack or the others as they took off over the hill. Screeching with victory, several faeries landed on the wheel, working as one to steer the ship. It drew to a stop right over Jack's head, the ramp at his feet.

"Nothing they won't do for nectars," Xeno said. The doctor chuckled. "Right then. All aboard!"

CHAPTER TWENTY-TWO

From Ashes & Flame

IND WHIPPED AND SLAPPED AT Jack. He grinned into it, steering the ship for Londinium. Below, Beth manned the cannons, cheerfully ready to take aim at any of the rest of the fleet foolish enough to follow. Alongside the ship the faeries soared, passing the bottles between them until not a drop was left and they flew in drunken, crooked lines.

At the other end of the deck, Xeno and the doctor argued in hushed voices. Jack strained his ears hard as he could, so that they actually moved on his head, far back as they would go. But still he couldn't catch more than the odd word.

"Tell him!" That was the doctor.

"Matters not a whit . . ." And Xeno.

Ahead, with the aid of his binoculars, Jack saw the spiky roofs of Londinium, its towers and turrets, factories and steam. Footsteps approached; Jack kept his metal hand on the wheel and turned to Xeno, the crack in his eye looking out over the horizon.

He cleared his throat.

"*Mephisto*," Xeno began in a slightly sharp voice, "seems to think that seeing as we've got this far, we should have a wee chat."

"What about?" They couldn't stop now; that would just be daft. And he was close, so close to being able to get home.

"Well, see, we've got to build the thing first, of course. Put it back to rights, poor creature. But if Sir Lorcan *is* using it to keep himself alive, as is clearly the case, and it summons its soul back . . ."

"Lorcan will die," said Jack. "Yes, I know." He *hoped* so.

Xeno's face cleared. "Told 'im you were made of strong stuff. You can go home knowing you've done a fine thing, young Jack. We'll all be better off without that man, with his whisperin' and whatnot in the Lady's ear. And we'll 'ave the Gearwing back."

The Empire had needed him, after all. No one else had discovered the secret of the Gearwing. Even to Dr.

Snailwater, who was very clever, it had been only a myth. But he wasn't meant to stay here forever. A home of his own waited in London, full of Mother and Father and Mrs. Pond, who would be so proud of the things he'd learned here.

"Steady now!" cried the doctor. Londinium was beneath them, the first scattered hovels coal black in the night. Around them the faeries cheered, or at least Jack believed so. It was a bit hard to tell with faeries. The melting Thames rippled, a great steely ribbon flung across the city, and beside it the clock tower rose to needle at the sky, the top hidden by clouds.

Jack slowed the airship. The wind died a little in his ears. Gas lamps behind the clock faces beckoned them, a lighthouse on land. So close, he could see the individual flames behind the thick white glass, a dozen of them fuzzy and flickering. *Tick, tick,* went the Gearwing's feathers, counting the minutes.

"Going up," he said to the others. Beth had joined them and stood at the prow, hair streaming behind her. Choking, blinding fog swallowed the airship whole, so Jack couldn't even see his hands on the wheel. It soaked his clothes with filthy drops. He couldn't breathe, could only hold the wheel with all his might. The world spun around him and he didn't know which way was up or down.

Suddenly, the masts pierced through the thickest of

the cloud, letting in streams of moonlight, brighter and brighter until the whole deck was lit with it and glorious air filled Jack's lungs.

"Everyone all right?" the doctor asked. Jack nodded, turned to look at the others. Xeno held fast to a railing. Beth, completely unperturbed, hadn't moved an inch. And there, right before them, was the enormous iron bell that would never ring for this clock again.

Closer, closer. The wooden hull nudged against the stone tower, and Xeno lowered the gangplank, sprinting across it with an armful of heavy rope. The faeries formed a wide circle all around the tower, wings flapping, ready to pounce on any who came their way.

Tethered to the thick columns at two of the belfry's corners, the airship rocked only a bit in the wind. Beth skipped into the tower, causing the doctor to clutch at his heart before he edged with slow, cautious footsteps, weighed down with his sack of tools. It was really a very long way up; Jack's stomach knotted tighter with each step, relaxing only when he landed on the solid belfry floor.

The greasy smell of the clock room made Jack feel ill. He'd spent a great deal of time imagining the Gearwing trapped here with it, each tick a tiny scream. The doctor handed out tools, and Jack, who had the deftest hands, skin and metal alike, crawled beneath the mechanism with a turnscrew. The constant motion above filled his head.

"We're saving you," he told it, which made him feel better even if it couldn't hear him.

Again and again, they filled Dr. Snailwater's sack with pieces. The ones that were too large were carried between Xeno and the doctor, carefully up the winding staircase and over the plank. Sweat beaded on Xeno's brow as he hauled the escapement up through its hole in the floor, hand over fist on the thick cables.

Silence, deafeningly loud, filled the room. The clock had stopped ticking.

This would be the thing. Many times they had wondered whether Lorcan would feel this moment, sense it with the magic he'd used to steal lifetimes. Jack was sure of it. Somewhere in his exile, this was the moment Lorcan would know and would surely set sail for Londinium with every haste.

Time, now that it wasn't being measured, seemed to speed up. The four worked faster, wiping eyes with grimy arms so as to see the tiny slots in the heads of the screws. Hands were wiped on rags when they slipped on bolts thick as thumbs.

"That's the last," said the doctor, and it was. All that remained of the clock was a dark smudge of grease spread over half the floor. "In here, leastways."

He was worried. Jack knew why, but it'd be all right. It *had* to be all right.

Though Jack himself was a little worried, too.

Rust-red metal covered the deck of the ship, bright, yet dull at the same time in the moonlight. The faeries giggled and pointed, but Jack did not laugh. He took the wheel and prepared to hold his breath, ready to descend through the miasma of cloud.

"Ready," said Xeno. The ship began to drop. It was easier this time, knowing the disorientation would come, but still Jack was relieved to break free, gasping and cold though he was.

"Oh, don't be such worrywarts," said Beth when Jack had pulled the ship to a stop, the bottom of the ship level with the clock's westward face. "You'll put me back together if I fall, won't you, doctor?"

"Of course, dear," said the doctor in a hoarse whisper.

She knotted a rope about her waist, the other end tied to the sturdiest mast.

Jack looked over the ship's prow, regretting it immediately. At once the ground seemed very far away and near enough to be terrifyingly solid. Beside him, the doctor shook with nerves.

Oh, he couldn't watch. Jack squeezed his eyes shut, so as not to see the moment she climbed onto the railing and jumped to hang below the ship.

"All right," she called up. "Close as you can, please, and quick before I lose a shoe." Jack brought the side of the ship flush to the tower, the fingers of his metal hand crossed in a wish.

But she did not fall. The rope did not break. Piece by piece, she removed each feather marking the minutes from the first face, slipping them into a satchel around her neck. With a larger turnscrew, she pulled free the long, copper hands, the tail feathers of the magnificent Gearwing, so nearly alive and no longer a myth. Beyond the sentineled faeries, the sky was lightening. Together, they hoisted Beth back to the deck to empty her arms and the satchel; then Jack steered the ship carefully around to the next face, then the next and the next. A mountain of feathers grew, weather-dull, razor-sharp. When the last one dropped atop the pile, the four gathered around it, looking at one another for a moment.

Every last part. They were ready.

They flew westward through a faery storm, the sky clogged with the creatures until Xeno called to them and thanked them for their assistance; it had been very useful, thank you very much, but here, take more nectars and be on your way. Now Jack could see, and he steered the ship for the spot they'd chosen, deep in a thick forest just outside the city, where the ship could hide among the trees.

Landing was only slightly tricky. The bottom of the ship snapped branches, sending tiny steel birds into shocked flight. It scraped against rocks, bouncing about until Jack felt fizzy as a bottle of champagne, his head about to pop right off.

"That'll do," said the doctor. He and Xeno busied themselves with ropes, throwing and tying until the vessel was properly moored. It hung just a little ways in the air, enough to open the ramp and leave, should they wish to.

None of them wished to. Jack wasn't even sleepy, though he'd been awake a very long time. The fingertips of his normal hand itched to begin; the tips of the others felt like they did. The doctor ordered him into warm, dry clothes and to eat some bread and cheese, washed down with tea made in the ship's galley.

"I . . . I . . . ," said Beth, her eyelids fluttering. She sat down, her back against the railing, beneath a branch furred with leaf buds.

"Leave her," said the doctor. "We'll wind her up again in a bit." Jack's hand stopped an inch from her key.

"The soul needs rest, even if the body can thunder on like a steam train," said Xeno. "There's beds below if you—"

"No, thank you," said Jack.

The doctor chuckled. "Not surprised. All right, lad, this is your show." He waved a hand at the gathered pieces, hundreds of them, perhaps thousands. Chilly doubt crept into Jack, but if he gave up now, he would never get home.

And they didn't have much time, if Lorcan knew.

Jack walked among the parts, careful not to tread on a single one. Just in case. He was good at this, he reminded himself. Hadn't he always known just how to fix the gramophone or the bellpull without even looking in a book?

He thought of Beth, broken on the tables.

These long pipes, those were legs, yes. And the shorter ones, for the joints of wings. He began to separate the pieces, just as they'd done in the workshop, gathering them in groups. Hoping he had the faintest clue what he was doing. The doctor ran about, taking measurements and jotting them down in a notebook, muttering.

Xeno had been right; the talons, which had been tucked away in the back of the clock, looked like nothing else. By the first pinking of dawn, the feet were assembled and attached to the legs. The deck was hard beneath him as he sat for hours, squinting, comparing bits side by side. Xeno and the doctor brought cups of tea that grew cold, bread that hardened to rocks. His fingers slipped with oil, and when his normal hand grew too stiff with ache to turn another screw, fix another rivet, the doctor took over, then Xeno, who wasn't as skilled at this sort of thing, but who knew the story of the Gearwing best.

"Can I have a go?" Beth asked, freshly wound, bright as the morning around them. Jack gave her two bits he thought were meant to go together to form the back, where the wings would attach.

"Will you be sorry to leave?" she asked.

He blinked at her, surprised she'd ask this sort of question. "A little, I think," he said.

"It's been a grand adventure, having you here." She tilted her head to one side, the turnscrew still in her hand. "It's been . . . very nice. And p'raps you're not that ugly."

Jack felt himself go slightly pink.

The sky was light by the time Jack realized he'd made a mistake, a wing crooked and wrong. The wrench sailed halfway across the ship, taking a good-sized chunk of a mast with it. Eyes burning with shame and tiredness, he ran down into the belly of the ship and curled himself next to the gently humming engine. Footfalls sounded on the stairs, but he tucked his head to his knees and didn't look up.

"I had a daughter, once," said the doctor. "She took the fever and died, and her mother with her. I wasn't a doctor in those days."

Jack blinked. Waited.

"Didn't think I'd lost my hand messing about with medicine, did you? And I didn't lose it like yours, neither. Nay, I ran a factory back then, making all the bits that make up other bits. Everything, all the gears and widgets and sprockets and whatnot, having to be exactly the right size to fit together. Not so very different, I suppose."

No, not so very different. "But you're a doctor now," said Jack.

"Indeed. But too late to save my own girl, or my wife. I help others nowadays, and made Beth's sisters, then Beth herself. And she's my daughter now, you might say, though very much her own person, despite her shortcomings. Which, truth be told, are *my* shortcomings."

"Why are you telling me this?" Jack asked. He didn't mean to be rude, but sometimes it couldn't be helped. He didn't understand.

"Because, lad, there's naught I wouldn't give, or do, to spend one more day with my family. And here you are, a stripling of a boy who has already survived the worst this land can throw at a body, but suddenly ready to give up after one mistake?" Dr. Snailwater's voice grew fierce. "You should be grateful some things can be fixed."

"What if I can't?" Jack asked in a small voice.

"Then you try again!" The doctor took a deep breath. "Come on, now. Goodness knows it's been a long day, and we're maybe all a bit fractious, but you've come this far."

Stiff, sore, Jack got to his feet. The doctor patted him on the head.

On the deck, Beth and Xeno were hard at work. The shell of the Gearwing stood at the prow, missing its innards but the shape of the thing was there, beakless head to neck, spine to legs. Talons curled into the floor. A ladder leaned against the railing. Wires snarled in Xeno's hands, and someone had fixed the broken wing.

Jack knelt, searching. This piece and this one and this one. Cogs and gears to spin, thick copper bands. He rummaged in the tools for what he needed. Both the doctor and Beth stopped what they were doing to watch the heart begin to form. Jack concentrated; it had to be perfect, parts placed just so. Only when he was sure did he stand and walk slowly to hang it inside the creature's chest.

"Good chap," said Xeno quietly, holding the ladder for Jack, who held it in turn as Xeno put its stomach below and threaded the thin pipes that would carry oil. "Close it up and feathers next." They covered the body with big copper plates from the clock, caught its eyes before they rolled away across the deck.

And now for the feathers. Straining, sweating, climbing the ladder to reach the highest bits, they worked until the deck was clear of every scrap of metal. "I believe you should do the honors," said the doctor, proffering the assembled beak, awe etched into the lines of his face. Xeno's eyes glowed with the light of belief confirmed, not dulled even a little by the crack, but Jack couldn't shake the sense that it looked like a statue of a thing, rather than the thing itself. There was no life to it, no spark. Hope and fear warred within him.

It had all been real. The story couldn't fail him now. He looked up at the Gearwing, a magnificent phoenix just like in his books, no less alive for being made of metal.

"I'll hold the ladder," said Beth. "Oh, this is exciting, isn't it?"

Jack climbed. Ever so carefully, he affixed the beak to the bird's face, the hinges closed but ready to open in song. His hand trembled as he reached for the key—at its neck, just like Beth—and began to turn.

And turn.

And turn again.

Finally, it would go no farther. Everything was a held breath; the breeze stilled in the trees, the birds silenced.

An eye moved. Then both. Slowly, the beak opened.

And the Gearwing began to scream. Oh, it was not a pretty song at all, as the story said, but an awful screeching that made Jack turn loose the ladder to cover his ears. It pierced right to the very center of his brain as he fell to the deck with a bone-jarring *thump*.

But still it did not stop.

"What's the matter with it?" Jack shouted, but nobody

answered, whether because they couldn't hear him over the screaming or because their own ears were covered, he didn't know. The enormous wings spread and flapped, gears turning slowly, then fast and faster. Its feet left the deck and it flew in panicked, dizzy circles, still making that horrendous noise, crashing into the masts and the trees beyond the ship.

Just when Jack thought he would rather die than listen for another second, something happened, something that had left him alone since the night he put a stop to the hangings.

The voice came. But it was not Lorcan's this time. It was loud in his head, somehow louder than the scream.

Help me, the Gearwing begged, raspy, metallic, a deep sound with sharp edges. *Please, help me.*

CHAPTER TWENTY-THREE

Lorcan's Return

WHEN LORCAN AWOKE IN THE grip of fever, it took him several long minutes to remember where he was. Ah, yes. The mountains, for the Lady no longer loved him. But she would again; she would. He had all the time he could ever desire in which to wait for her forgiveness. This was nothing more than the blink of an eye, the quick flutter of a wing.

On shaking legs, he rose. "Trinket!" he tried to call, but no sound came from his throat. Water, that was it. Cool, fresh water and he would be perfectly fine. But this was the fever, affecting his mind, and as he drank from the jug Trinket had filled from a stream, the water evaporated to steam on his lips. Desperate, nearly blind, he felt his way back to his bed.

Hours later, he awoke again. The ship rocked gently to and fro in the breeze, tilting his stomach with each movement. He put a hand to his chest to feel the heat there, the fire that raged within.

But something was wrong. Something more than the nonsensical sickness. Illness never took him; that was for common people. Mortal people.

His heart was not beating, and this could mean only one thing.

"Trinket!" he called, and this time, blessedly, his voice worked enough.

"Master?"

He required . . . He required . . . "My things, Trinket. A hair."

"But there are no more, sir," said Trinket. Of course, there hadn't been for many days, he remembered now. None of the Lady's long, dark, beautiful ones, none of the short locks snipped from the boy at the palace. But he did not need to see in order to know.

The clock was broken. It did not tick, minute by minute, and so his heart was still, as still as it was when he ventured through the doorway, to the London where the clock's magic did not work. He touched his burning cheek, imagining that he could feel the flesh there rotting beneath his fingers. How much older would he look were he to glance in a mirror?

He didn't care to find out.

"We must go back," he said to the imp. "Ready the ship."

"But, sir, you are—"

Lorcan grabbed the thing, threw it with all his might against the wall. Its own crude repairs to itself did not hold; it fell to pieces on the floor.

No matter. There were always more where it came from. The Empire was overrun with the things. He must return to fix it. Perhaps get a glimpse of the Lady, simply to assure himself that she was perfection as ever. And then he would retreat again, just as she wished, to wait.

Shaking, stumbling, Lorcan dressed. Suit, a necktie of crimson silk, his topper. Nothing must seem out of place, should he be seen. No one must suspect that anything was the matter.

Daylight blinded him on the deck, with no clouds this far north to dull it. He withdrew his dark glasses. Ah, better. His pocket watch infuriated him with its ordinariness, its stubborn determination simply to tell the time.

But it was all right. Within hours, he would be back in Londinium.

CHAPTER TWENTY-FOUR

The Egg of Fire

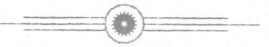

"ALL RIGHT!" JACK SCREAMED, UNABLE to hear his own voice. "All right, we'll help you!" They already *had* helped it, in point of fact, but he didn't think now was the time for quibbling.

The noise stopped. Jack's ears rang. The fantastic Gearwing returned to the deck, its feathers whining against one another as it settled its wings.

"It can't summon its soul," growled Xeno. "He's trapped it somewhere. I'm sure of it. As if turning the creature into a bleeding clock wasn't bad enough."

Beth frowned. "It's not inside him, like mine?"

"No." Xeno's hands curled to fists. "No. A mere body wouldn't be enough to stop the call. Too many holes, y'see.

He had to make certain that if someone ever reassembled it, it still wouldn't be itself."

Hatred blazed to life again inside Jack. "Can it *find* its soul? I mean, if we tell it to fly away?"

"Likely not. Perhaps if we get right up close, but it's confused. Being without a soul is an extremely disorienting thing. Surprised it managed enough to ask for help, frankly."

So they had heard it, too. The Gearwing stood statue-still again, as if it'd never moved at all. Xeno paced the deck, muttering to himself. "'Course he did. 'Course. Dunno why I didn't think of it. Keep it close enough that he can use its power, but not so close it fights with 'is own. Keeps it safer, yes."

Jack's heart sank. He'd been so clever to discover the clock's secret, but that was a bloody great tower in the middle of Londinium, right where he could see it. The soul could be anywhere the length and breadth of the island or beyond. He didn't know how close it would have to be, and he doubted Xeno knew, either. The Gearwing was unique, special, not a ten-a-penny faery giggling its way around the Londinium slums. He pictured a swirling soul in a corked brandy bottle, buried a half-dozen feet in the dirt, or hidden in a cave, or weighted down at the bottom of a river.

He'd come so close to going home; it had never seemed quite so far away as it did now. His normal hand was callused, cracked, crusted with blood from unnoticed scratches, and his head ached from lack of sleep.

"How large would it be?" the doctor asked Xeno, who rubbed his chin in thought, leaving a strip shinier than the rest. Absurdly, Jack wondered if he polished it every day.

"About as big as a sheep, I reckon," said Xeno, quite serious. "A youngish one, mind. Not your full-grown ram."

The doctor raised his bushy eyebrows, but nodded.

"He'd want it somewhere he could see it," said Beth decisively. The other three looked at her in surprise. She shrugged. "The clock was, even if it was still a bit hidden at the same time. So he's hardly going to pack the soul in the back of a broom cupboard, now, is he? It'd make him feel all clever-like, to have it right out there in the open, not looking like what it is."

She was right, of course. Jack grinned at her, and Dr. Snailwater patted her absently, but a leaden darkness descended upon them as, together, it occurred to them that even this narrowing down didn't help a great deal. "Somewhere he could see it" meant Londinium, presumably, but Londinium was full of nooks and crannies, rooftops and tunnels through which the trains chugged.

Though underground didn't seem likely, anything was possible. He remembered Xeno's insistence that he believe that, the first time they met.

"Perhaps we ought to wait for night," said the doctor.

Xeno scoffed. "That will do precisely what good, eh, Mephisto? We won't be able to see a blind thing."

"Is that better or worse than everyone seeing us, hmmm?"

Jack ignored their bickering and looked at the Gearwing again. It hadn't moved, not one flick of a feather. Warily, he walked up to it, afraid that any moment it could panic again. Poor creature, indeed.

"Don't be afraid," he told it. "We're going to fly. A different sort of flying than you're used to, I expect, but it'll be all right." Did he imagine the glimmer in its eye? He hoped it was there, that somehow the Gearwing understood.

"Worry not, lad." The doctor rested a hand on Jack's shoulder as Jack took the airship's wheel. Clearly he'd lost the argument. "We'll find it."

He was only trying to cheer Jack up, Jack knew, but it was a nice thing nonetheless. Particularly since the doctor hadn't even believed in the Gearwing until a few days before. It felt like months. Months since he had eaten or slept, months since that warm, laughter-filled supper at the doctor's house after Beth was back together.

And much, much longer since he'd been home, safe in his room with his toy soldiers to guard him, which he was sure were the only kind worth having. Forever since his mother's laugh had drifted, tinkling, up from the dining room below.

The ship rose from the trees, leaving behind a very boat-shaped dent in the forest. Everyone—bar the Gearwing, of course—held on as Jack swung it about to aim for the city. There was some truth to the doctor's worry of being seen. Jack wished they had the faeries again, but they were out of nectars, and good luck trying to get faery help without them.

So, alone, a single ship in the sky, they flew back to Londinium. In daylight, the outskirts were even shabbier, crumbling shacks built of splinters, spit, and prayers, filthy factories, scrubby fields of blackened, coughing goats. He wished his pockets were full of coins that he might shower down to the people, but he wasn't rich here.

And he had his eyes on the city, peeled and searching as it whizzed past underneath them.

It could be *anywhere.*

More clouds had come in since they'd snuck in like fiends to steal the clock in the dead of night. He flew below, looking, looking. . . .

He needed his binoculars. Well, technically the doctor's binoculars, but they fitted Jack's eyes just so. After some searching, Xeno unearthed them and strung them around Jack's neck.

Jack lifted them. The empty clock tower looked close enough to reach out and trail his fingers over the stone. The faces were hidden, but none on the streets would be using it to tell the time regardless. No, it had been just for Lorcan.

"What's that?" asked the doctor, pointing. Breath caught in Jack's chest, but it was only a red dress on a washing line, billowing in the wind. Xeno took the wheel so that Jack might look properly.

"It's no use," said Jack, dropping the binoculars, which whacked him painfully in the chest. "Go up. Hide above the clouds. I need to think."

More horrid, cloying fog. He knew to close his eyes, hold his breath, but still it was awful, cold and wet and swirling. Above, the air thinned and cleared and Jack gulped it gratefully. The empty clock faces stared at him. He spun to check the Gearwing, but it was still as it had been since it landed on the deck. It showed no sign of knowing it was so close to its prison.

Somewhere old, because Lorcan was. That was no help in the slightest. *All* of Londinium was old; Lorcan and the others before him had built this one to be just like Jack's London because it amused the Lady. And he'd taken the great clock tower and twisted it into something horrible, evil, when in London it was a beautiful thing, beloved by everyone.

Somewhere old and *famous*. Though this, too, wasn't as much of a help as he wished. London was the greatest city in the world, known to all. He pressed his hands to his eyes. "I don't know," he said, dejected. "Back down, I suppose, and . . . and along the river." He pressed the binoculars to his eyes the instant they were free of the clouds, the masts still dragging filigree patterns in the lowest of them.

Something caught his attention. He'd already moved on to the next patch of the city and jerked the binoculars back.

He'd seen before that it was different here, but *why* was it different?

"There." Jack pointed. "Why is that an egg here?"

The doctor grasped the binoculars, nearly throttling Jack, who was far too excited to care about silly things like breathing. The stone column rose from the ground, not as high as the clock tower, but Jack could still remember the sickening climb to the top with Mrs. Pond and standing on the narrow platform there.

"Why, that's the monument to the birth of the Empire," said Dr. Snailwater. "S'posed to be a copper dragon's egg or somesuch. I've never looked particularly close, myself."

No, no, that was wrong, though Jack was sure Lorcan had been vastly entertained by his little joke. Replacing the urn on the monument to a fire that had raged through half of London. A *fire*.

Funny, too, to force a creature that could live forever into the horrible tedium of counting each second of it.

"Jack," said Beth.

It was in there. He knew it. He—

"Jack," Beth said again. "Would you like to know that Sir Lorcan's coming?"

He looked up. She was pointing, out past the gleaming egg to the airship beyond.

Jack's heart hammered. Time seemed to stop entirely. With the binoculars, he could see Lorcan, neat and pressed as ever, flanked by cannons large as two men. But there was something else, too, something that filled Jack with a secret joy.

Fear. Lorcan had spotted the Gearwing.

"Hurry," Jack shouted. "We must get to the egg before he does. Hurry!"

In the belly of the ship, the engine roared louder and the ship leaped forward, Xeno grinning at the wheel. Jack couldn't take his eyes from Lorcan, close enough with the binoculars to see his pale face and eyes glinting red.

A rage such as he had never known swept through Jack. Lorcan didn't care about anyone but himself and the Lady, and he'd turned into a wretched thing who wasn't bothered who he hurt to get what he wanted.

They were over the river now, sailing above its curve, every inch the airship traveled matched by Lorcan's coming closer.

"Faster!" Jack shook. "We need to go faster!"

The doctor took the sails to steal every scrap of wind. Lorcan disappeared from Jack's sights, and Jack cast the binoculars about, desperate to find him. And there he was, a spectral figure behind a billow of steam.

"Cannons!"

Xeno spun the wheel with a violent jerk. The airship tilted, everything not nailed down sliding dangerously on the deck.

"Beth! Get down below where you'll be safe!" the doctor commanded. He would not be able to save her if she fell in the river to rust before they found her. The cannonball missed, only just, whistling past, plummeting to a splash loud enough to reach them in the sky.

The egg was a hundred and fifty feet away. A hundred. So intently was Jack watching it that he saw, too late, Lorcan's ship speed up and sweep around the monument.

The deck pitched as Xeno tried to get out of the way.

He didn't quite manage. The world turned inside out. Splinters rained down to the water as the whole ship quaked from the blow. Jack fell into the railing and tasted a mouthful of blood, pain searing his nose. Frantic, he looked for the Gearwing. Some deep-buried instinct to protect itself had caused it to jump from the deck to fly in blind circles overhead. He could feel its terror clawing at him.

"Mean business, do you, *Sir* Lorcan?" Xeno shouted. "We'll just see about that!" He pulled the ship about to bear down on the other. The doctor swung across the deck, clinging to the sail.

But Jack had seen where Lorcan was taking aim. "No!" he screamed, running toward the Gearwing, but it was too high above him. *Move*, he thought with all his might. *Move!*

Below, something rumbled. Steam swallowed Lorcan so Jack could see only the very top of his hat. Any second now an enormous ball of iron would smash into the bird, and surely it would be too bent and broken for anyone to fix ever again. The deck shook under his feet, and an explosion tore the air.

Beth had fired first. The cannonball tore into the hull of Lorcan's ship, knocking it off kilter. Enough. Just enough for his own shot to miss the Gearwing's beak.

"Oh, good girl!" the doctor roared. Jack grinned through bloodstained teeth. He would thank her later.

"You will not defeat me, little Jack!" Lorcan's voice crossed the distance between the ships. "You may have discovered my secret, but I have lived your lifetime many times over, and I will not let you ruin it!"

Jack's eyes cut to the Gearwing. It had landed at the other end of the deck, rage and terror and confusion pouring from it like oil. The Monument was starboard, two hundred feet. The airships were nearly nose to nose and there was nowhere to go, no room even to turn around.

Oh, yes, he would ruin Lorcan. His one normal hand gripped the railing. He would ruin Lorcan and then, then he would go home. Xeno turned his head, and Jack caught the corner of his eye, pointing up.

Xeno winked.

Air whooshed past as the ship shot up into the clouds. Jack choked and coughed, but within seconds they were free, of the fog and of Lorcan.

"Everyone all right?"

"Yes, Doctor! Xeno, the egg, please!"

The ship spun like a top and sped off. Behind them now, Lorcan had joined them above the clouds, but they had distance. Enough? Jack wasn't certain. But he hoped. Another blast of cannon fire burst; this time Lorcan's aim was not so unlucky. It slammed straight into the ship, and Jack lost his hold.

It was like flying without the ship, like having wings. Jack soared into the air, buffeted, tossed, but there was only so far he could rise before the fall must begin. To have landed on the deck would have been bad enough.

Thick as the clouds were, they would not break his fall, cushion him with their false softness.

Wildly, with no time to think, Jack flung out his arm. His brass fingers caught the edge of one of the holes in the side of the ship, and he hoped that Beth wouldn't choose this one from which to fire another cannonball.

"Lad?" the doctor shouted, terrified. His bushy hair appeared over the railing, relief coloring his face as he saw Jack, clung to the side of the airship like a barnacle.

"It's all right," Jack yelled at the top of his lungs. Every breath scorched them with cold. "The egg, get me to the egg!"

Beth's face appeared from inside the ship. "Hello, Jack. Gosh, what are you doing out there? Shall I pull you through?"

Jack shook his head. The hand Dr. Snailwater had made him held fast to the wood, not tiring nor slipping, the way a normal one might. His feet braced against the side of the ship as they dropped back down through the clouds and the great copper egg shone twenty feet away . . . Ten . . .

The doctor's head appeared again, eyes wide with fright and worry.

"Closer!"

Five feet. Four.

"Closer!"

Jack closed his eyes. He took a deep breath of the Empire's soupy, sooty air.

And he jumped.

All the wind knocked from him as he landed on the egg. It wobbled on its plinth, held there as a jewel might be held to a ring. It was smooth, polished so his face, bloodied and bruised, looked back at him.

Reaching down to grab the fattest part, Jack wrenched the egg free, letting them both fall to the narrow platform that circled the column. He hit the stone and folded, rolling over. The egg slipped from his arms and skittered away; on his knees, Jack crawled to catch it.

Only then did he look up, right into Lorcan's eyes. His ship hovered in the air, and on the deck Lorcan was entirely still for a moment. He raised his hands, imploring.

"We can discuss this, Jack. Give it to me, and I will teach you magic of which you have never dreamed. Magic far beyond what you have seen in your time here in the Empire. I will show you all my secrets. We shall rule together, the Lady's sons."

Jack looked at his feet. He had once stood in this very spot, in London, with Mrs. Pond. He glanced over to the other ship, battered and struggling, where Beth, Xeno, and Dr. Snailwater watched. Xeno gave Jack a tiny nod. Behind them, the Gearwing stood, and this time it wasn't fear Jack felt from the bird, but a hope that rang clear as the bell for which it had once measured the hours.

Very deliberately, Jack carried the heavy egg to the railing. For a moment he held it there, high above the solid ground at the base of the column, and then he let it tumble over the side.

CHAPTER TWENTY-FIVE
The Sorcerer's Final Words

WHEN LORCAN SAW THE EGG drop, a great resignation came over him. Since he'd stolen the Gearwing's soul, it had occurred to him only in times of great worry that someone might discover his secret. Now he was left without even the leisure to wonder how it had come to pass at the hands of this young boy who still reminded him so of the Lady, with his dark hair and mischief.

He supposed it did not matter.

The egg tumbled from the boy's hands, over the railing, spinning, catching what little light the Empire had to offer and creating much more of its own.

On the other ship stood the bird. Tall and proud, but

not gleaming. Not yet. A collection of parts put together, measuring time in a different way than it had as a clock.

The Gearwing could not escape time, but it could reuse it. Over and over.

The Lady's face pushed all other thoughts from his head. Really, it was very like her to demand his attention. His life had been devoted to her; it was only fitting that his death should be, too.

"She will be so alone," he whispered.

He sensed the egg smash on the ground below as much as heard it.

Lorcan fell.

CHAPTER TWENTY-SIX

The Gearwing's Gift and the Flight of Fire

T HE EGG CRACKED ON THE cobbles and exploded into flame, a great ball of it, yellow and orange, red and gold. The Gearwing opened its beak. Jack prepared to cover his ears, but the music that came now was the sweetest song, filling his head and whole body with warmth. Awed, he watched as the Gearwing unfurled its wings and rose up into the air. The flame rose, too, a fiery streamer, flicking, flashing until the Gearwing caught it and swallowed it down.

A crowd had gathered on the street, drawn by the battling airships. Whispers passed among them, but Jack couldn't think of a single word. Fire rippled over feathers, restoring them to shining copper and brass, steel and iron.

The very sky seemed to lighten, the air grow warmer, and a wide grin took over Jack's face. Joyfully, the bird flew, stretching out to half the size of a proper dragon, soaring and diving only to rise again.

Thank you, it said.

"That's a fine thing," said the doctor, dabbing at his eyes. Beth was smiling, but that was Beth. Xeno steered the ship up to the edge of Lorcan's, the hulls knocking against each other. Xeno lowered the airship so Jack could climb aboard, his long, strong arms reaching to keep Jack steady.

"We should get the other one, too," said Jack. He didn't want it to drop from the sky right over the city.

"Good thinking, that chap." The ship rose and flew over to Lorcan's, the hulls knocking together. Xeno held it steady so Jack could climb from one to the next.

Lorcan lay on the deck, bloodless, shriveled, gray. Rotted bones, the skin melted from them. A few wisps of colorless hair sprouted from his head. His topper had rolled away. Making sure no one was watching, Jack gave the body a tiny kick, enjoying the last short time in which there was no Mrs. Pond to tell him he was being spiteful. The bones under his toe crumbled to dust, caught on the wind and disappeared. A pair of dark spectacles slid from a pocket of the sagging suit, and Jack thought he finally understood that small mystery. Bending over, he filched

them, quickly slipping them away where they wouldn't be seen.

"Ready when you are, lad," the doctor called over.

The Gearwing flew alongside the ships, flashing like a shape glimpsed in a hearth fire. Cheers roared up from below at the return of the Gearwing, Londinium's greatest legend, back to give them hope again. Word had traveled fast, running from one street corner to the next. It looked as if all of Londinium had turned out to see it.

It really was magnificent, the Gearwing, all shreds of its life trapped as a clock gone, its soul restored. It swooped about the two ships, as if checking Jack, Beth, Xeno, and the doctor were all still there, its beautiful song filling the sky.

They steered the ships to land in the gardens on the river embankment, a place laden with yet more memories for Jack. The damaged airships tottered and rocked unsteadily but landed well nonetheless.

"Jack!"

His feet back on the ground for the first time in a great many hours, Jack turned to find the source of the voice. He knew that voice. Arabella ran over the grass, mussed, her pointed face the picture of amazement.

"Word came to the palace," she said, her breath only a little strained. "The Lady sent me to find out what all the fuss was. They said an airship—" She stopped. "Well, it 'ad to be you, didn't it? And, oh, good gracious, that's never what I think it is?"

"Now, now, Arabella," said the doctor, approaching on slightly wobbly legs. "Everyone knows the story of the Gearwing."

"Oh, my word. *You* found it? Oh, my word."

Jack led her to a bench, shooed away the faeries perched there, lest they get any ideas about hair pulling, and told her the whole tale.

"'E's . . . dead? Truly? For forever?"

"For forever," Jack agreed.

A smile threatened to split her face. "You're a fine boy, Jack. And you were a fine son to the Lady, whatever she may've said at the end."

"Will she be all right?" he asked.

"Don't worry your head over that." Arabella stood. "I'll make sure of it."

Dragonfaeries with their elongated wings zigged and zagged over the thick river water when Jack joined the others. The Gearwing ceased its circling and came to land before them, towering, aglow with life. It raised a copper leg to point a talon at Jack, who stepped forward.

I owe you a great debt, said the Gearwing. *You have but to tell me how to repay it.*

Jack told him. The great bird spread its wings and

sparks crackled along the metal feathers. They gathered to a single, red-hot filament that flew into the air, twisting, snapping, flying in the direction of the clock tower.

It waits for you. Whenever you are ready.

"Thank you."

The gratitude is all mine, young friend.

The Gearwing backed away, hinges flexing, cogs spinning. Once again it raised a sharp talon, but not to point. Metal scraped against metal as it drew the claw down the center of its chest, the edges of the tear curling back, and hooked its heart like a fish. There was a terrible screeching and the thing came free, dangling from its foot for a second before it flew through the air to land in Beth's hands.

Jack opened his mouth to scream, but found he could not. Great wings unfolded, the gears biting at one another with long teeth, and Jack knew, somehow knew what it meant to do. He ran to the spot where it stood, but it was already gone, away over the water, and he could only watch through wet eyes as it gathered its light, flame licking over copper. All along the river, the people of Londinium shouted and cheered. Behind Jack, Xeno clapped his hands and whooped.

It exploded like a Chinese firework. Piece by piece, the Gearwing they had so carefully put together rained down on the river in a thousand splashes.

Jack wheeled on Beth, a lump in his throat. "Why did it do that? Did it ask you what you wanted?" As it had asked him. "Did you tell it you wanted its heart?"

"Don't be daft." She rolled her eyes, but there was a sadness in them, as if the heart she held had already begun to take hold of her. "I didn't do anything. Thought it gave only one miracle. It asked *me*." Beth looked down at the heart in her hands. "It asked me to look after this until it comes back. So's no one else can do what Lorcan did."

The doctor put his arm around her. Xeno bent so his glass eyes were level with Jack's.

"You know the story, Jack."

"But it was . . . Everything we did! All for nothing!"

"Oh, no." Xeno shook his head. "It's survived worse than this! Think on it. You've seen worse with your own eyes. It's a legend, and you take it from me. Legends don't die nearly so easy as people. The Gearwing will return when the time is right. You mark my words."

Jack walked a short ways away. The Empire of Clouds was churning, busy, coughing up steam. And so it would keep doing, long after he had gone, and just as London must have done in his absence.

"It's just sad," he said after a while. Xeno patted him on the shoulder.

"You think so?"

"Why, don't you?"

"Look around you," Xeno said gently. Jack looked at the faces of the people lining the streets and the water, happy in a way he'd not seen, not his whole time here. "You brought it back to us when we thought it was gone forever. It has to die so that we can have hope it will live again."

Together, they walked the short way to the clock tower, empty save for its bells. Beth slowed to fall into step with Jack, the doctor and Xeno ahead. The crowd parted for them, looks of awe and even fright on their faces, but Jack felt a hand or two pat him awkwardly on his back.

"She'll love me now," said Beth. "I'll be able to love her back, and I'll live at the palace, and Dr. Snailwater will visit me to take my creaks out when I need it."

Jack stopped to stare at her. Her eyes glowed, but not an angry red like Lorcan's once had. A friendly, warm gold.

She smiled sweetly. "It only makes sense. She can't die, and I can't, so we'll be together for a long while. Until the Gearwing needs this again, leastways. That's better than nothing, isn't it? She'll dress me in pretty dresses and be nice without Lorcan about the place making her all wretched."

"Oh, Beth," he said. A yawn cracked his jaw. He thought he might even sleep well on the blankets in Dr. Snailwater's parlor, but the best bed of all waited for him in London. Just on the other side of a doorway.

They neared the door at the bottom of the tower—still wood, but it glowed red around the edges at Jack's approach. Now that the time had come, he had no earthly idea how to say good-bye, or thank them for the help.

"It's all right, lad," said the doctor. Xeno shook his hand, a proper shake between men, and Beth, holding her heart, gave him a quick kiss on the cheek. He wiped it on his shirtsleeve. He grasped the handle and, with one last look at the great, seething Empire, opened the doorway.

CHAPTER TWENTY-SEVEN

London

O N THE OTHER SIDE OF the door, the sun shone, a ball of flame. Tears pricked Jack's eyes, but it was rather nice to be right about the spectacles. He slipped them on, the lurid brightness immediately dulled. Much better. Now he could see the busy street beyond the gates, packed with snorting horses and the carriages they pulled.

The gardens where he'd last seen Mrs. Pond were mostly empty; sunny as it was, winter still clung to the city with frosted fingertips. High above, the longer hand of the great clock swept slowly from one minute to the next. Pressed to the railing beside the river, he watched the boats, decks lousy with their captains and merchants. No hints of bronze or brass or steel winked up at him from the shallows picked clean by mud larks.

The clock chimed half past the hour.

It was a few minutes to the edge of the park where he'd first encountered Beth, a few more along to the spot where her birdcage should have been, but wasn't. Lords and scullery maids bustled about, not a single brass grille in sight on their noses. The birds that sang in the trees were flesh and blood, but perhaps no more alive than the other sort. Jack would miss them, the fantastic creatures, Beth, Xeno, Dr. Snailwater. Even the Lady, who'd been kind to him for a time. But Beth would love her now, and the Lady would love Beth in return. They'd sort out the bit about the cake somehow.

Here, in this London, the compass worked. The needle spun, making up its pointed little mind, and decided on which way was north. Jack curled his clockwork hand in his pocket—he was going to have a grand time showing *that* to Mother and Father—and set his feet to Mayfair.

To Mayfaer and the Mayfaeries!

Not quite. But it was home.

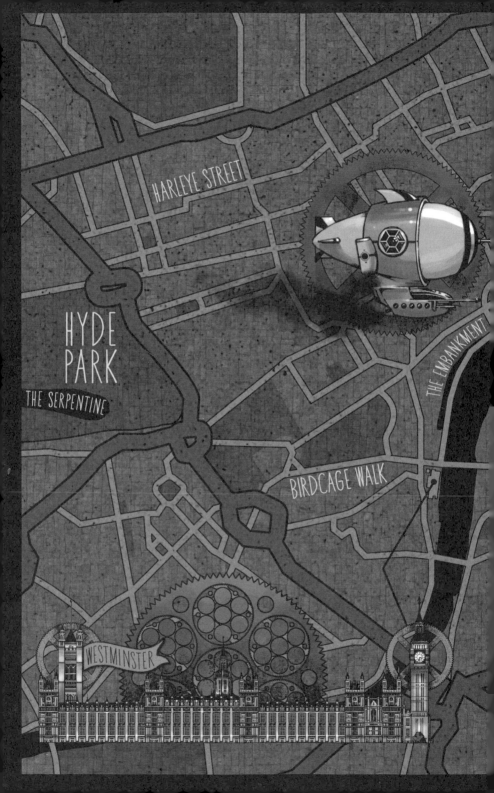